Times Two

Brian Musselwhite

TIMES TWO
Brian Musselwhite

ISBN 9781914615443

A CIP catalogue record for this book
is available from the British Library.
Published 2022 Tricorn Books, Aspex
42 The Vulcan Building Gunwharf Quays
Portsmouth PO1 3BF

Printed & bound in the UK

Times Two

Brian Musselwhite

To my family, Sue, James, Charles, Claire, Will and Art and my friends Penny, Judith and Carol, many thanks for their help and encouragement.

Times Two

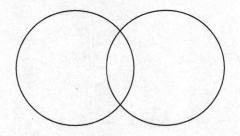

Part One

Chapter One

On the occasion of his thirty-second birthday in 2081, not long after his partner of the last six years had finally ended their relationship, Lucas Mallon finally came to a decision. He would travel back exactly 100 years - he had always had a preference for round numbers. Since the new technology for backward time travel did not allow for any shifts in space, he chose to centre his journey in the place where he lived just now - an old house in Gomer Lane, near one of the few remaining open spaces close to the sea that remained in the Gosport district of the Solent City conurbation.

Lucas was a highly competent social researcher, one of the youngest professors of Sociology at the University of London. Only a tiny group of such specialists were permitted to undertake experiments in the newly developed science of time travel. These few, including Lucas, were permitted to spend no more than six months in a different time period in history for the purpose of preparing a full and truthful report on aspects of social history in past times. His particular assignment, chosen as a result of a lengthy discussion with the head of the experiments at the Wells Institute, the eminent historian Dr Michael Boone, was to be a study of local involvement in organised social groups. Of course, thanks to twenty-first social media, there was an abundance of history to be studied from data from mobile phones, uploaded videos, blogs, vlogs and all the rest. But though these sources gave some insight into the past, they were basically a haphazard, subjective and random collection. Even on the local history sites, many of the posts purporting to give truthful information concerning life a century ago were flawed or even totally incorrect. After all, no-one writing today had actually been alive at that time, let alone having any memory of "the good old days". Lucas thought it would be a wonderful opportunity to actually witness and take part in the life of the past.

Before embarking upon this exciting adventure Lucas was equipped with all the items deemed necessary for survival in the twentieth century. The Institute provided him with an NHS number, a driving licence, contemporary maps of the area and large amounts of banknotes and coins from the 1980s. He spent six weeks at the Institute studying idioms of language, attitudes, general behaviour patterns and news events of that time. He had decided to stay, for a little while at least, at a quiet hotel called The Alverbank when he travelled back in time. In 2081, this particular building was still in existence although these days it was a retirement home for centenarians and was the centre point of a gated community surrounded by modern buildings: houses, shops, a leisure centre and a couple of restaurants.

Lucas thought it would be helpful in his research project if he chose to join one of the social groups which were in existence in 1981. From an internet search he discovered that there were several groups in Gosport which produced shows for audiences- there were two theatre clubs, a pantomime group and an operatic society. As Lucas possessed a reasonable good singing voice, he finally decided that he would join the latter group, which was called "The Gosport Operatic Society", when he arrived in 1981.

During the first week of November in 2081 Lucas underwent his final psychological and physical tests to ascertain his fitness to undertake the project. Before he received his final briefing from Professor Boone and the small panel of time travel physicists at the Institute, he used the time travel machine - named "Mallett" after its original inventor - to travel back in time a few minutes. He was told to stand on a marked spot alongside the tall tube attached to a glass casing. Not being a scientist, Lucas had very little idea of how the apparatus worked - he knew it was something to do with circulating beams of laser light. But the short experiment was successful. At the start, he had a feeling of weightlessness, and heard a noise like a sudden rush of wind. Later, after the process had been reversed, the professor told him that he had travelled back in time five minutes, and then had been brought back to the present.

"When you travel back into 1981,of course you won't actually have to be here in the Institute to use the Mallett machine," Professor Boone told him. "We have devised a remote controller that will link to the apparatus so that you can access it wherever you are. This gadget will also show the date upon which you must return and will have a countdown screen, as the timing of your transfer back must be totally synchronised with the Mallett machine."

In common with very many people in the late twenty-first century Lucas was thoroughly self-disciplined in the arts of mindfulness and meditation. These skills had always enabled him to slow down any racing thoughts, to calm both his mind and body and relieve him of anxiety and negativity. As a result, after he had put his present life on temporary hold, he was able to relax in the days before his adventure was to begin and he awoke from a deep and untroubled sleep on the morning of Monday November 10th.

Chapter Two

Methodically Lucas packed everything he might need into a large old-fashioned suitcase. He put on his already prepared antique clothes - how strange they looked and felt! - and strapped the vital remote device into an inside pocket. At mid-day a trusted driver from the Institute arrived to collect him from his house and took him the short way to the seafront. The driver dropped him off near a small copse - a safe and lonely spot where he knew he would be unlikely to be observed. Lucas breathed deeply, taking a final view of the familiar world of 2081 He took out the remote device and checked that its already programmed dial read November 9, 1981. He closed his eyes and pressed the small button. There was that feeling of weightlessness again and the sound of rushing wind.

He opened his eyes again. The time machine had worked. The buildings that he had been able to see a moment ago were no longer there. For a moment, he found it hard to marshall his thoughts. Was he really standing here at this moment in the past?

Picking up his suitcase, he began to walk slowly towards the little road that led to The Alverbank. The air he breathed felt indefinably different to that he was accustomed to in 2081 as he crossed the little bridge that led to the venerable old hotel. The first thing he noted, with some amusement, were the ancient cars parked outside the building. The interior of the hotel was certainly old-fashioned - probably, he thought, even for 1981. But Lucas rather liked the look of it. He found the old wooden panelled walls and the antique chairs quite charming. At the reception desk, a smiling young man greeted him and booked him in to stay. Lucas signed the register, putting as his address "care of University of London".

"Thank you, sir," said the young man, "I hope you had a pleasant journey here."

"Ah, yes, really it was quite an easy trip!" replied Lucas with a smile.

As he carried his suitcase up to his appointed room, Lucas reflected that it seemed very strange to have just spoken to someone from a century ago. He was fascinated to see the room that would be his home for the next few weeks. Everything in it was so old! But there was a decent sized writing desk and the bed felt comfortable enough - and the view out over the large lawn with a glimpse of the sea beyond was superb. Slowly he unpacked and then rested on the bed for half an hour.

Lucas had deliberately chosen to arrive in 1981 on a Monday because he had discovered that that was always the day of the week that the Gosport Amateur Operatic Society held their meetings. In the hotel, he chose afternoon tea rather than the full evening meal as he wanted to be at the society's rehearsal for a whole evening. To pass the time, he went out for a stroll along the sea front. Here it was not so easy to believe that he really was back in 1981, for the coastline itself had hardly changed in a hundred years. There were not many people out and about on this cold November afternoon. Of course, he had seen videos and photographs of people in the twentieth century, but it was fascinating to see them for real. A pleasant-looking young man in the company of an elegantly- dressed woman nodded a friendly greeting to him. As they passed by, Lucas reflected sombrely that neither of them would live long enough to see his own time. Yet here they were, at this moment as alive as he was!

Every now and then, a car or lorry passed by on the narrow coastal road. Lucas was very aware of the petrol and diesel fumes emanating from these ancient-looking vehicles. In his own time, all transport was powered by the much cleaner fuel of electricity. But he knew he would have to get used to the polluted atmosphere while he stayed here. And it had come into his mind that perhaps he ought to buy a car to enable him to travel further afield - always supposing he could learn how to operate one.

Eventually he retraced his steps back to The Alverbank in time for tea. Soon he was seated in the dining room, wondering whether or not the food would taste very different to that to which he was accustomed in 2081. But when the food arrived - four cheese and ham sandwiches with a generous helping of salad - he was pleased to find it delicious. Soon afterwards, heartened by this pleasant experience, he went to his room and made his first observational notes, writing them down rather laboriously by hand into a small book, reflecting as he did so that in this age before the internet had become common that he would have to get used to the old methods of recording and research without the aids of his all-powerful twenty-first century devices. Not long after seven, he put the notebook away and changed into the casual clothes he had brought with him, hoping that his outfit would be appropriate enough for a social evening in 1981.

Chapter Three

Having thoroughly memorised his street map, Lucas walked through the dark streets towards Stoke Road and the David Bogue Hall. On the way, the residential areas were much as he knew them in his own time, but Stoke Road was almost unrecognisable. Instead of the low-rise flats and the pedestrianised retail and business centre, here in 1981 were some simple small shops and a scattering of houses, alongside a dimly-lit road quite busy with ancient cars At last he managed to find the David Bogue Church and Hall, a typical building of the 1960s long since vanished in 2081. The hall itself which was used for the group's rehearsals was part of the church building. He located the entrance, hesitated just for a moment and then pushed open the door and walked along a short corridor into the hall itself. Inside there was a pleasant hubbub of conversation. He saw about forty people of various ages. A few were on the stage, dismantling the sets from a recent production. Others were standing about in groups chatting and a few of them looked across towards the newcomer. A tall man walked over to Lucas, smiling pleasantly.

"Hello!", he said, "have you come to join us? I'm Andrew, I'm the musical director." Lucas introduced himself and remembering the polite custom of the age, offered his hand. "Come and meet some of the members," said Andrew, leading him across to a small group in the middle of the hall. "Lucas! Meet Patricia, Belinda, Beth.....Bob,

Vernon and Barry. And this is our producer for our next show, Andrea."

The introductions made, Lucas soon found he was quite enjoying the bright chatter. As a newcomer, he was the centre of attention. "I hope you'll be staying!" cried Belinda, "we always need new men!" "Well, you always need a new man," said Patricia tartly. "Good to see you, mate," said Barry, "you know we're doing *H.M.S. Pinafore* next - it'll be good to have you on board. Tonight we're just packing away the stuff from our last show, but we'll be starting "Pinafore" on Thursday. Care to come to The Vine for a drink later on?"

Lucas agreed readily. He was having an interesting time so far - he had already met some friendly people and was enjoying the liveliness of the conversations. A little later, Andrew introduced him to the rehearsal pianist, June, and asked him if he could audition for the men's chorus. "If you have a copy of 'Pinafore' could you possibly try out one of the songs - any one - and sing it on Thursday?"

"I'd be glad to," replied Lucas, "I hope I'll be good enough to be in the show."

"Don't worry," said June, "as usual, we're short of men, so really, so long as you can stand up, you'll be in!"

It was half past nine, and people were beginning to leave. Barry came over to Lucas. "OK for the pub then?" he asked. So he joined a group of about a dozen and walked round the corner to The Vine. Entering the pub, he was amazed to see how it looked inside. In his own time, places of refreshment tended to be spacious, brightly lit and almost clinically tidy and clean. By contrast, this place was dark, hot, cramped for space and the air was beery and smoky. "Find a seat, I'll get you a drink - what'll you have?" asked Barry.

Although Lucas had studied the habits and tastes of this period, he was rather unsure about what primitive drinks were available. But he remembered that beer was a very popular beverage in the twentieth century, so he decided it would be a safe bet to request one. "A small glass of beer, please," he replied. For a moment Barry looked puzzled. "Ah - a half then? Bitter?" he asked. "Er, yes, thank you," answered Lucas a little nervously. Barry went off to the bar and Lucas joined a small group at one of the tables.

Chapter Four

Lucas was quite the centre of attention. Andrea wanted to know whether or not he had been in a singing group before. Belinda asked him whereabouts he lived. Heather inquired as to his marital status. He explained that he was staying in Gosport for a few months and that the University of London, where he was a researcher in social studies, was paying for him to complete some special studies. The University had temporarily arranged for him to stay at The Alverbank, but he told them that he was hoping to find a flat or some other accommodation in a little while. While he was talking, Barry, Vernon and Bob brought drinks over to the table. What a contrast, thought Lucas, to bar services in 2081! In his own time, it was usual for drinks to be ordered from a device set into the tables which were then swiftly delivered on trays powered by small drones! As the conversation flowed he learned a good deal about the group and its members; and, indeed, trained as he was in social observation, a good deal about the folks round the table too. Barry was a thoroughly decent and hearty chap. Vernon had a wry sense of humour. Bob waved his hands around while he was talking. The women were interesting too. Blonde Belinda was openly flirtatious. Andrea, the producer of the next show, had an air of self-confidence. Heather talked nineteen to the dozen. Beth was quietly spoken and, Lucas thought to himself, rather more intriguing than the other women. He found her rather attractive and began to speculate as to whether she was interested in him. Somehow, when he was preparing for his adventure, he had not imagined that he would experience any particularly strong subjective thoughts, trained as he was in cool, analytical objectivity. But the sheer exuberance and the feeling of living life for the moment that emanated from these people from past times was infectious. He was thoroughly enjoying himself.

At the same time another part of his mind was recording some fascinating facts that he would note down later. For example, unlike everyone in 2081, these people in the pub had not yet had the benefits of the social media platforms such as Facebook, Twitter and suchlike. They knew nothing of the internet. They did not even have mobile phones. He wondered if perhaps these inventions which were still to come had had the effect of reducing the "personal level" of conversations in his own time. Naturally he also noticed that both men and women in the group, and indeed throughout the pub, smoked cigarettes. Even though he had known that this would happen in these bygone days before health and safety issues had banned this practice altogether, he could see the pleasure the smokers were having from their habit. As for the drinks - he found his glass of beer tasted rough, and he supposed that the wines and spirits favoured by some of the group would probably be harsher to the palate compared to the carefully synthesised beverages of 2081. At one point in the evening, Lucas remembered that, as was customary at the time, he should offer to buy a round of drinks. Having memorised the orders from the people he was sitting with, he went up to the bar. He found it not only annoying but incomprehensible to have to wait to be served by either of the busy barmen. When at last he was asked what he wanted, he watched the barman dealing with the drinks in what he considered to be a most unhygienic way, but understood that that was obviously how this type of thing went on in 1981! He managed to sort out the right amount of unfamiliar money rather than paying with his personal credit card which he would have used for every transaction in 2081 and struggled back to his new friends with the drinks. Beth and Belinda had asked for a sherry, and he had decided to try the same for himself. Back at the table, he tasted this unfamiliar drink - how potent it felt!

A little later, Lucas needed to use the "Gents". This was another strange experience. How primitive this necessary room seemed! Cold air blasted through a hole in one of the barred windows. The sinks had real bars of soap, rather than the liquid dispensers he was familiar with. He looked around in vain for the infra-red hand dryers before he realised that the only method of drying his hands was to use a rolling hand towel.

But he was soon enjoying the chatter and laughter round the table again, and was quite sorry when he heard the call of "Time, ladies and gentlemen, please! Drink up now!" Soon everyone was preparing to leave. As they went outside into the cold November night, Barry asked Lucas if he wanted a lift back to The Alverbank, but he declined the offer as he was looking forward to a walk and a chance to relive his experiences of the evening. He knew he was going to enjoy being part of the Operatic Society and he was already looking forward to Thursday's rehearsal.

Chapter Five

Lucas slept well enough in the hotel room on his first night in 1981. Next morning, after eating a really tasty breakfast in the dining room, he made a few notes about his experiences of the night before. He found himself thinking about the impressions the different people he had met had had on him and wondering about what their lives were like. He wondered what they had made of him. On the whole, he decided, he had made a good start to living in the past - although the antiquated washing and toilet facilities in the hotel room would take some getting used to.

Today he was going to visit the town that he knew so well in his own time. He knew there would be many changes; after all, he had looked at several images of Gosport that had been taken over the last hundred years. But when he had walked through Stoke Road to reach the town centre, he was fascinated to see how it really was in 1981. He walked slowly down the High Street, passing by what appeared to him to be a random and varied selection of shops. A road ran right through the middle of the street, full of cars, lorries and vans while cyclists weaved their way between the traffic. There were quite a few people walking around, and Lucas realised that not one person was using any form of mobile device. Of course they weren't, he said to himself, this was 1981, years before these things became ubiquitous, but it was still strange to see. He reached the harbour. Here, everything was completely different. Instead of the elegant bridge across the water that he knew in 2081, there were ferry boats. A bus station obstructed the view of the sea. There were two enormous blocks of flats, long demolished by his own time. Compared to 2081, the town looked as though it had evolved without any type of planning at all. The Gosport that he knew so well was a very different place. During the middle of the twenty-first century, a lot of money had been spent to try to create a more leisurely place, with plenty of open spaces and the utilisation of its natural seascapes. Its historical heritage was also brought to the fore -the various sites were easily accessible for young and old alike by means of driverless vehicles of every type. The quieter charms of Gosport had been developed as a contrast to the bustle of the mega-city of Portsmouth on the other side of the bridge.

Nevertheless, he soon began to enjoy looking round the town. He was surprised to see so many different types of shops, although of course this was long before people began to do their shopping on line rather than in the High Street. He went into Woolworth's, a store whose name he recalled from his studies, and was fascinated by the sheer amount of different goods that were on sale there. In a newsagent's, he bought the local evening newspaper and a simple, cheap wristwatch - his own smart one didn't work in these old times. Glancing at the window display of a shop called Rumbelows, he was amused to see the selections of ancient television sets and radios, all rather expensive considering their old-fashioned simplicity. Waiting at a pedestrian crossing to cross from the south side of the street to the north side, he overheard a woman standing nearby remark to her friend, "Oh, all this traffic - isn't it a nuisance!" Lucas knew that the High Street was due to be pedestrianised a few years later; and he also knew, from reading posts written on the local history site some years later, that many believed that banning High Street traffic had been a big mistake, leading to the town's decline. Even in 2081 there were many people who moaned about Gosport not being as good as it used to be. He remembered a quotation from Doug Larson, the American columnist: "Nostalgia is a file that removes the rough edges from the good old days."

Lucas was enjoying the hustle and bustle of the High Street as he observed the individuals and groups going in and out of the shops. At lunch time, he decided to try a meal at the Wimpy Bar - a type of little cafe that was long gone in his own time. Untidy, slightly scruffy as it was, there was an air of cheerfulness about the place. Most of the items on the menu seemed strange to him, but he chose a Wimpy Grill which was obviously very popular in these olden days. Rather to his surprise, he found the food delicious. For afters, he selected an ice cream concoction called a 'Brown Derby' and enjoyed that too. The whole meal, supplemented by two cups of tea, cost a mere 63p. As Lucas sorted out his old coins to pay the bill, he reflected on the massive rate of inflation that had occurred In a hundred years. In 2081, there were no "pence" any more, nor had there been any for many years before. The pound was now the most basic unit of currency. For a basic lunch similar to the one he had just eaten he would expect to pay at least £50.

In the afternoon, he decided to have a look around to

see if he could buy a few items of clothing - he had not been able to bring much on his trip across the years. He visited the Co-op department store, Millett's, and finally Burton's, choosing shirts of different styles, socks and underwear. In Burton's, he picked out a pair of brown cord trousers and a large overcoat. He realised that in these old days he had to retire to a booth in order to try on the clothes - in his own time, "smart" technology could adjust clothes to ensure a perfect fit.

Weighed down now by his various purchases, Lucas decided he would take the bus back to the hotel. At the bus station he collected a timetable from the little shop on the concourse and discovered that he should take the No. 9 service which passed along Stokes Bay. After he had waited a while in the draughty surrounds, his bus arrived and he boarded the ancient-looking green vehicle, still finding it a novelty to pay by cash instead of using his personal credit card. The journey was bumpy and not particularly comfortable and the bus was noisy and smelly, but somehow he felt quite exhilarated to have a ride on a vintage vehicle.

Chapter Six

Back at the hotel, Lucas decided that this evening he would stay in and take the full evening dinner that was on offer. After taking his new purchases up to his room, he rested for a little while before coming downstairs to the small but pleasantly furnished dining room. He was impressed both by the service and the meal itself, which consisted of asparagus soup, a cold pork salad with creamed potatoes and buttered turnips and, to finish, a selection of cheese and biscuits. Afterwards, just like any other hotel resident, he took a seat in the comfortable bar - quite a contrast from the crowded and noisy place he had visited yesterday evening - and sat with a glass of wine at hand to read the local paper he had bought in town. Accustomed as he was to be able to access news stories both local and international at the touch of a button, he found the perusal of a printed newspaper somewhat cumbersome at first. Eventually after glancing over some local reports he discovered an announcement of a play - a famous old piece called *Blithe Spirit* - which was to be performed by the Thorngate Theatre Club from Wednesday to Saturday. This would be another opportunity to see a performing group and its interaction with an audience, so Lucas decided he would go and see the show at the Thorngate Halls on the next evening.

Back in his room later, he reflected that so far his travel back in time had been really quite successful. He had already accrued plenty of material on the subject he had been sent to examine and what was more, now he was beginning to get used to these old fashioned times, he was finding the experience most stimulating. He had hardly missed his normal life of 2081- this was a holiday with a difference!

Chapter Seven

After breakfast on Wednesday morning, Lucas went out walking to explore the nearby area that he knew so well in his own time. First he walked up to Gomer Lane. There was his house! How very strange and somehow rather moving to see it as it was in 1981, obviously quite new in this time. In 2081, his house, now over a century old of course, was secluded from its neighbours and the road by several trees and bushes, but here its aspect was quite open. He wondered who lived here at this time. But he could hardly knock at the door and introduce himself as the future owner of the house!

After a moment or two he walked thoughtfully along towards the roundabout. He was surprised to see open fields and spaces nearby, for in his own time all of this area was heavily built-up. There was a garage on one corner of the roundabout, basically a filling station but also with a few cars for sale on one side. Lucas amused himself for a little while by looking at these strange-looking vehicles. It occurred to him that it might be a good idea to buy a car - if he could work out how to drive one - to save him from having to walk or use public transport all the time he was here. Certainly, in 2081 he was accustomed to much easier ways to travel anywhere.

For now, he carried on walking along the main road to Lee-on-the-Solent. How quaint and quiet this little place was in 1981! A century later it had become a really popular and busy seaside resort, offering hotels, leisure and shopping arcades, a casino and major facilities for water sports of every kind. But on this cold November day there were few people about. Lucas found the gentle slowness of pace rather pleasing, used as he was to the crowds and bustle of holidaymakers whenever he came here in 2081. He spotted a couple of little cafés in the small Art Deco block near the seafront - buildings that should really have been preserved, he thought, for they were long gone by his own time. Both cafés seemed rather similar but he decided to try lunch in "The Penguin" this time, reserving a visit to "The Bluebird" for another occasion. Taking a seat with a pleasant view out of the window, he ordered an old-fashioned meal of egg, sausage and chips - such fatty foods were rarely seen in 2081 but he found the meal absolutely delicious! As he ate, he glanced around the cafe to observe his fellow diners. Quite a few of them were elderly. He had noticed that the menu was offering cheaper dinners to 'O.A.Ps', a term no longer in use in the twenty-first century after there had been a long campaign to remove any form of discrimination on the grounds of age.

After he had finished eating, he left the cafe and took a walk around the little town. As he had seen in Gosport, there was a large variety of different shops, most of them including greengrocers, butchers, hardware suppliers and a couple of clothing stores owned and run by local people in those days before the large national concerns took over. He glanced into the interior of quite a large hairdressing salon, thinking as he did that eventually he would have to have a haircut at some time during his stay.

Eventually he took the bumpy bus ride back to the hotel and after having a light teatime snack, got ready to visit his second local performance group, this time as a member of the audience. At seven o'clock he set out for the Thorngate Halls, a large Georgian period building which in his own time had been preserved as an administrative block for the Gosport Superhospital. When he arrived, he was very interested to see that in 1981 that the venerable building was quite separate from the hospital, which of course was much smaller at that time. Just inside the entrance, he found a stand containing many leaflets advertising the many groups which met during the week at this place, all under the aegis of the Gosport Community Association. Lucas collected quite a few of these for future reference and possible participation.

Lucas bought a ticket and a programme and entered the theatre. The room was almost full - he reckoned there were as many as two hundred people there. Waiting for the play to start, he was aware that his seat was not very comfortable. The room was rather cold, and the surroundings seemed rather shabby. But he quickly became absorbed as the play began and was impressed by the standard of the acting. Whenever he had seen a live performance in 2081 the action on stage was so often enhanced with three-dimensional holograms, spectacular lighting effects, fully immersive sound and other technological additions. But the comparative simplicity of this production seemed to add a particular feeling of intimacy between the actors and the members of the audience.

At the end of the performance, he hoped he would be able to make some contact with members of the group. He joined several members of the audience who were making their way to a room in the building named "The Georgian Bar". Waiting to be served at the little bar, he gathered from the conversations around him that many of these people were friends or family of the cast. Soon some of the performers came into the bar, greeting people that they knew. He recognised one of the men who had been on the stage and introduced himself, explaining that this was the first time he had seen a Thorngate Theatre Club play and how much he had enjoyed it. The actor, who was called Clive, told Lucas that the group performed three times a year and had put on many different types of drama. He went on to say that Lucas was welcome to join the group which like the operatic society, met for rehearsals twice a week. Once more, Lucas was very conscious that he was warmly welcomed. He moved around the room, chatting with many other members of the group. There was the same feeling of vitality and fun that he had already experienced with the operatic society on Monday evening but the difference tonight was the interaction between the actors and audience following an actual performance. He observed some interesting encounters. One of the younger members of the cast was in conversation with his obviously pleased parents. A young woman was laughing gaily with a group of others who were her work colleagues. A tall, rather dour- looking young man was standing slightly to the side of his wife or girl-friend, who had had a big part in the play, while she flirted with two other young men.

Walking back to *The Alverbank* after the bar had closed.

Lucas reflected on a most enjoyable evening, not only as far as his analytical research was concerned but also on a personal level. Once again he had been made to feel very welcome. It would have been good to have belonged to both the operatic society and the theatre club, but he didn't think he could fully commit himself to both at the same time.

Chapter Eight

On Thursday morning, he awoke from another comfortable sleep to a cold and windy morning. He decided he would spend most of the day recording his first observations and analyses for his assignment. He sat at the little table in his room, writing his report. It was so strange to write with pen and paper, as he had not brought any of his usual technological aids with him as he had known that they would not work in this period of the twentieth century. Time passed slowly and he only left his room for lunch and tea before getting ready for the evening's operatic society rehearsal. He dressed in his new outfit and once more walked through the streets to the David Bogue Hall. He was greeted cheerfully by several people as he went in.

"Good to see you, mate," said Barry, "come and have a seat in the back row with the rest of us baritones and basses." Presently, Andrew, the musical director, announced that they would have a sing through some of the choruses for the first half of the evening and then after the break any prospective principal could try out the audition pieces.

Lucas found the singing most enjoyable. Andrew was a good conductor and helped the chorus to achieve a pretty good sound. At half past eight Lucas joined the queue for tea and biscuits, paying the ladies who had provided it a mere ten pence. While he was chatting to Barry and

Sam, Andrew came across and asked him if he was ready to do his audition for the chorus. Somewhat nervously, he walked across to stand next to the piano, where June, the pianist, welcomed him with a smile. Lucas cleared his throat and launched in to the Captain's song from *HMS Pinafore* that he had been practising a little back at the hotel. During the song, some of the people broke off from their chatting and listened.

When he reached the end of the song, Andrew said, "That was fine, Lucas. We'll be glad to have you as a member of the chorus!" There was a murmur of assent from those who had been listening and Lucas, with a sigh of relief, sat down and prepared to watch as the various singers came forward to try out the songs that had been chosen as audition pieces for the principal parts. Beth was one of the prospective principals for the part of Josephine and Lucas found that her singing commanded his attention straight away. He thought she had poise and a fine voice. Patricia also performed the same song with some style, but not as well as Beth, thought Lucas. There were one or two others who he had not yet met trying out different songs. One was called Calvin, a pleasant looking tenor who was trying out the leading man's song, and another was Jacqueline who sang Little Buttercup's song. Barry, Bob and Vernon also practised some of the audition numbers

Chapter Nine

The rehearsal finished at a quarter to ten and Lucas joined a group on their way to The Vine once again. The night was very cold and Lucas felt happy when they entered the warm and welcoming pub. He felt more at ease this time as he stood at the bar ready to buy drinks for Belinda and Beth - this rather quaint old way whereby the men ordered the drinks for the ladies seemed to work quite well, he thought. The operatic group managed to find two adjacent tables and soon everyone was relaxing and chatting happily.

At Lucas' table were Beth, Belinda, Sam, Dennis, Jacqueline and Calvin and for a little while Lucas said little, listening to the conversations around him. He had always rather prided himself in his ability to understand body language. For example, he observed that Belinda appeared somewhat annoyed with Sam, who in his turn seemed rather downcast. Beth looked as though she was interested in Calvin, for she brightened whenever he spoke to her. Meanwhile, Jacqueline and Dennis were obviously enjoying each other's company, laughing a lot together. At one time, Andrea, the producer, came across from the other table to congratulate Lucas on his singing tonight and to welcome him to the chorus.

Belinda smiled across the table at him. "It will be really good to have a new man in the show!" she said brightly, At this, Jacqueline turned to him. "You want to watch her!" she laughed, giving Belinda a friendly nudge. "you being a handsome, single young chap - are you single, by the way?" "Yes, single and fancy free!" replied Lucas brightly. "How lovely!" said Belinda. "Most of us here are married, or attached!" "Yes, more's the pity," sighed Beth.

The conversations turned to different topics, and Lucas offered to buy more drinks for Beth and Belinda, but both of them insisted on paying their way. Belinda asked for a white wine, while Beth requested a schooner of dry sherry. At the bar, Lucas decided to try the dry sherry himself - causing the barman some amusement by asking for two 'scooters', never having heard of the term "schooners" before. When he returned with the drinks, Sam was offering his cigarettes round the table and he held out the packet to Lucas, who naturally shook his head. He had already observed however just how much pleasure the smokers round the table seemed to get from their habit! He was also beginning to feel the sense of flirtation that was in the air. He watched Beth as she drank her sherry.

She caught him looking at her, and returned his smile. She is really attractive, he thought. They held each other's gaze for a long moment before she said, rather conventionally, "Lucas,what do you think of the sherry?" He took a tentative sip of the unfamiliar drink and made a bit of a face. "It's rather strong!" he said. "Yes, but it has the required effect!" smiled Beth. It certainly did - raw as the sherry was, it gave Lucas an instant lift. No wonder it was so popular.

The conversation round the table turned to a discussion about the auditions for the principal parts in "HMS Pinafore" which were to be held on the coming Monday. "Lucas, you will come and see us trying for the parts, won't you?" asked Jacqueline. "I will," said Lucas, "I'm looking forward to it - you were all so good tonight!" "Oh, isn't he just the gentleman!" laughed Belinda.

All too soon, the landlord called time and they all made their way outside into the cold air. Lucas stood for a moment with Belinda and Beth before they set off to their cars. "See you Monday!" said Belinda. As the girls turned to go, Beth squeezed his hand briefly before she walked away. Lucas stood still for a moment, realising that Beth had slipped something into his hand. Excited, he hurried along to the nearest street light and unfolded a little piece of paper from his hand. It was a note with a simple message: "RING ME TOMORROW?" Underneath was a phone number.

Lucas walked back to the hotel, his mind in a whirl. Could it be that Beth really was interested in him? When he had contemplated this trip into the past it had never crossed his mind that he might be anything more than a coolly detached observer of life in 1981, engaged in gathering data for his special area of research. Yet almost at once he had become involved with the spontaneous feelings of flirtation and excitement that emanated from the operatic group. How strange it all was - being involved with people of a century ago! But he knew he wanted to be part of this contemporary scene. He also wanted very much to see Beth on her own.

Chapter Ten

Next morning Lucas awoke feeling refreshed and full of anticipation after last night's events. The weather was grey and bleak but he felt the joy of being alive on this day so far back in the past. After breakfast he strode out of the hotel and went for a brisk walk along the bay, before turning inland to Alverstoke village. It did not look so very different to the place he knew in 2081. The little cottages and shops, overlooked by the impressive St, Mary's church, were a familiar sight. He discovered a small cafe and went in to order a coffee. While he was enjoying his drink, he wondered at what time he should phone Beth. He had no idea of her domestic circumstances, but he understood that she was married and assumed that her husband would very likely be at work during the day. I'll phone her at about three, he thought. He wasn't exactly sure what he should say - he supposed he was going to arrange what they called a "date" in these olden days. Would this be the right thing to do, morally, he wondered - but he knew that he wanted to see this fascinating woman on her own.

He sat in thought for a while longer, drinking another cup of coffee and enjoying an excellent cake. It occurred to him that he could pass the time by having a look inside the church - he had never actually been inside it in his own time. He entered the church through the South door and was immediately impressed to see the fine stained glass window above the altar. Here too was a list of all the

Rectors of Alverstoke dating back to 1290 .This, together with all the history that this church contained, seemed particularly apposite to Lucas in his capacity of time-traveller. The words of the twentieth century writer, C. S. Lewis, came into his mind: "The present is the point at which time touches eternity."

Chapter Eleven

His thoughts troubled him somewhat as he walked back to the hotel. It was hardly morally right to ask a married woman to meet him in secret. Yet at the same time, the heady and exciting experience of the night before could not be denied. Right or wrong, he knew he really wanted to see Beth on her own and hope for developments in their relationship. At The Alverbank, he ate a light lunch and then took some time to study the ancient pay-phone that was situated near the lobby. There was a tatty notice which gave instructions on how to use the device. He worked out that he had to dial the number, wait for the person on the other end to answer and then feed coins - at least ten pence - into a slot before pressing the button labelled "A". Further instructions warned that beeping noises meant that more money had to be put in the slot to carry on the conversation; and if his call was not answered, he must press button "B" to retrieve his coins.

Unsurprisingly, Lucas found all this quite bewildering, accustomed as he was to making calls with a single touch on his ever-present mobile in 2081. But at last, having made sure he had plenty of the old coins to hand, he carefully dialled the number that Beth had given him. After a moment he heard her voice and remembered just in time to insert the money and press the button.

"Hello, Beth, it's me, Lucas," he said, rather breathlessly. "Hello, Lucas!" she replied, in what he thought was a neutral voice. "Um, you said I should phone you," stammered Lucas rather inanely. "Yes?" said Beth at the other end. "Well, er, I would really like to see you, I mean, on your own - can we go out together for an evening?"

There was a moment of silence and then Beth said, "Yes, I think I would like that." "Beth, that would be wonderful - which day?" asked Lucas, feeling a little more confident now. "Well," she said, "there's no rehearsal next Thursday, but I could pretend there was one so I could go out. Now, I'd better go now - I'll talk to you privately on Monday and we can arrange it." "Oh, thank you Beth, that will be great, " said Lucas. "Are you ok Lucas? Asked Beth, "only, you sound a bit strange - anyone would think you'd never phoned anyone before!"

Without thinking, Lucas replied: "It's this strange phone - I normally only use my mobile....." "Mobile? What's a mobile?" queried Beth. "Oh, it's a sort of different make of phone," exclaimed Lucas, desperately trying to cover up his error before adding quickly, "so, anyway, I'll see you at rehearsal on Monday. And good luck with your audition!" "Talk to you Monday, then. Bye for now!" said Beth. "Bye bye Beth - and thank you!" he said, and thankfully put down the receiver. He felt quite shaky. The phone call had been really difficult - what a fool he must have seemed to Beth! He hoped she wouldn't change her mind about going out with him!

Gradually, he began to feel more relaxed. She had agreed to the date after all. But what problems these people of the twentieth century had with regard to communication! He had found it so difficult to talk properly to Beth over the phone. But perhaps this was why most people in 1981 were better at talking and exchanging ideas face to face.

In the early evening Lucas went into the small dining room to avail himself of the excellent evening meal. On another table sat an elderly couple, smartly dressed. Overhearing some of their conversation, he discovered that they were staying for a night in the hotel as part of their celebration of the man's 75th birthday. Later, in the bar, as Lucas was ordering a glass of wine, the couple came in and introduced themselves as Robert and Stephanie Johnson. They told him that they were back in Gosport for a nostalgic visit - it was twenty years since they had lived here, having moved to Devon in the 1960s.

"The area has certainly changed a lot since we were last here," said Robert. "Yes, I sometimes wonder what on earth it will all look like in the future!" exclaimed Stephanie. Well, thought Lucas, I could tell you exactly what it will be like a hundred years from now!

After exchanging a few more pleasantries, the couple sat down and Lucas felt he should let them be on their own. It was so strange, he thought, to have been chatting with these two people who had been born in the early twentieth century. He found himself hoping that Stephanie and Robert would at least live long enough to see the Millennium. For a few moments he was overcome with so many thoughts - in less than a week, he had seen and experienced so many things and met so many different people. How strange it was, he reflected, that he had arrived in this world as a unique stranger, yet now he truly felt he belonged here.

Chapter Twelve

Saturday dawned bright and sunny. Lucas was pleased to see that the weather was decent as he had made up his mind to observe some social interaction between performers and audience of a different kind - he was going to watch a local football match this afternoon at Privett Park between Gosport Borough and their visitors from Kent, Canterbury City. In 2081, the Borough club was still in existence and Lucas had occasionally been present to see his local team play. Privett Park was still there too, but in his own time it had been developed into Gosport's major sports and leisure facility. The football team now played its games on an artificial weatherproof pitch which was surrounded on all sides by enclosed stands where spectators could watch the games in dry and warm conditions. The Gosport Borough club still played in the Southern League and was now, like many other football organisations, was owned and run by a supporters' trust.

Back on this Saturday afternoon in November 1981, Lucas discovered that the ground looked very different. He paid his entrance fee of 20p at a quaint little hut near the entrance, and pushed his way through an ancient clanking turnstile to make his way into the ground. There was a fair sprinkling of spectators waiting for the game to begin. Some were seated in the old grandstand, which provided just about the only cover from the elements. The only other buildings were a brick-built clubhouse, a battered old caravan which dispensed refreshments and a small wooden hut which sold old programmes and other football memorabilia. It was a far cry from what he knew in 2081 but Lucas felt that somehow the sparse facilities provided a more intimate link between the players and spectators. As the game progressed, he realised that the fans quickly became engaged with the action on the pitch. He noted with some amusement the strange almost skin-tight shirts and shorts, the heavy looking ball and in particular the uneven and muddy pitch. He was quite astonished to see the players heading the ball - a practice which had been discontinued in the mid 2040s when experts had concluded that this aspect of the game could cause severe brain damage in later life. He did not think the players looked as fit or as skilful as in his own time, but there was no doubt about their efforts and he was as happy as any of the other locals when Gosport scored a goal just before half-time. The spectators were absorbed by the unpredictability of the events on the field and Lucas felt that they were fully focussed in actually watching the game, whereas in his own time the electronic display boards showing instant replays of the action, team lists and advertisements acted as a distraction.

At half-time Lucas went to the refreshment caravan. A smiling woman took his 5p coin and handed over plastic beaker of hot tea. How strange it was, he thought, to have to add the milk from a large metal jug and then use a very elderly spoon to extract some sugar from a packet to complete his drink. However, old-fashioned as it was, it tasted good and he welcomed its warmth on this cold day.

The second half of the match took place under the rather primitive floodlights, which made a strange buzzing sound. The game itself was quite exciting, finally ending in a 2-1 win for the home side. As the final whistle blew, the players trooped off to applause and cheering from the spectators. Lucas left the ground along with many of the supporters and he was interested to hear their various comments and opinions about the game. It was quite obvious that they had enjoyed a shared experience of pleasure in being involved for a couple of hours in a small but important set of events - feelings that were common among all other local football fans throughout the country.

Chapter Thirteen

Back at the hotel, Lucas had dinner and then decided to spend the rest of the evening relaxing and watching the television in his room. He was still amused by the fact that there were only three channels to watch rather than the hundreds that were available in 2081. The little set in his room had no remote control, so he had to keep getting up to switch between the channels on the set itself. There wasn't much of a choice, he thought. ITV offered an old film, there was a programme about the aftermath of a crime on BBC-2 and a "chat show" called *Parkinson* on BBC-1. He watched the latter programme for a while, quite enjoying the banter between the host and a comedy duo called Cannon and Ball. Next on this channel was *Match of the Day* featuring highlights from a couple of first division football games. Lucas could not help thinking that the supporters of the higher-profile teams behaved quite differently to the fans he had seen a the local game - they seemed much more aggressive. He found the inane gesticulating and chanting really quite distasteful. Halfway through the programme, he switched over to BBC-2 to watch the news summary. Here, he found the coverage of the day's events quite simplistic compared to the in-depth treatment he was used to in 2081, although he had often considered that the constant discussions and analyses of the news in his own time was overdone. Tonight's news stories included rioting and a murder in Northern Ireland, a massive fire in Bolton Town Hall and a gas explosion in Bristol that destroyed two houses.

Grim events indeed - how much effect did such news have upon the everyday lives of those watching, he wondered? Perhaps, he thought, as he got up to switch off the set, less than in his own time, where world news was not only available twenty-four hours a day but was also discussed endlessly on all social media platforms.

Chapter Fourteen

After a good night's sleep, Lucas rose quite early on Sunday morning and went through his usual routine of a quick wash and a shave. How primitive his morning grooming seemed here in 1981 compared with the automatic hyper-hygienic rituals he was used to! However, as usual, he enjoyed his breakfast before setting out to Alverstoke church to take part in the morning service where he would be interested to observe another different type of social interaction.

There were few people out and about on this cold and windy Sunday morning. As he walked through the village Lucas noted that almost all the shops were closed, unlike in his own time when business went on as it did on any other day of the week. He entered the church in good time for the morning service, noting that the congregation was not particularly large. Most of the worshippers were a lot older than him and looked quite well-off, he thought. As the service began Lucas, who had occasionally been to church in his own time, found it all quite refreshingly simplistic. Church services in 2081 were enhanced with electronic screens, holographic imagery and surround sound but he enjoyed the straightforward nature of morning worship in 1981. He was impressed with the skill of the organist and joined in the hymns lustily. The vicar in his sermon expressed his sorrow over the continuing strife in Northern Ireland, leading the congregation in prayers for peace.

At the end of the service, he noted that many of the people shook hands and exchanged a few words with the vicar at the door. For many of them, he realised, this occasion obviously imparted a gentle sense of pleasure and comforting continuity and was an important piece of social interaction in their lives. Lucas decided to greet and thank the vicar too. The latter smiled pleasantly at him.

"Good morning! I don't think I've seen you here before," he remarked, as Lucas nodded in agreement. But then something strange occurred. The vicar, after shaking Lucas' hand, stood back sharply, saying in a low voice, "You have come from a long, long way away......this is so very strange....surely it cannot be possible......" And then, just as quickly, he smiled at Lucas.

"Forgive me, what on earth am I saying? You are most welcome to come again, young man!" And he turned to another couple of worshippers.

Lucas felt a little shaken by this encounter. Just for a fleeting moment, this man of God had sensed something different about him - had he realised that Lucas was not part of this world of 1981? Up till now, nobody else he had met had seemed to find anything odd about him. He walked away from the church and paced along by the sea road, trying to clear his mind. Fortunately the long walk in the cold air refreshed his mind. His metaphysical musings faded away to be replaced by the more mundane thoughts of what he was going to have for lunch.

He went to he Old Lodge, an attractive old Georgian

hotel. Inside, it was quite busy and he noticed two couples who had been at the church service enjoying a lunch. A waiter found him a quiet table near the window and presently Lucas was enjoying a particularly delicious lunch of steak with peppercorn sauce. Afterwards, while he was relaxing with a cup of coffee, he spent some time thinking about his life so far in 1981. He had been here now for almost a whole week. So far he had achieved quite a lot, he thought. He had observed at first hand a variety of social groups, although he had not expected to have become involved on a personal level. On this quiet afternoon in the pleasant and undemanding surrounds of the old inn, just for a few moments he began to feel a little homesick - for although he had prepared himself for feelings of dislocation, there was no getting away from the fact that he was in all reality alone in the universe.

But as he walked slowly back to The Alverbank, he told himself sharply to stand firm. He had chosen this path and there was much more work to be done - and plenty to look forward to.

Chapter Fifteen

After breakfast on Monday morning, Lucas sat in his room looking through the leaflets that he had collected at the Thorngate Halls last week advertising various clubs and groups. One of the daytime courses particularly interested him. This was the "Writers' Circle". Could he join it? If so, he thought, it would be very relevant to his studies, as well as providing a chance to meet some interesting and creative people. The group held meetings every Tuesday mornings, he read, and he decided to go along to the Thorngate Halls and see if it was possible to enrol.

It was a fine and brisk morning, and he enjoyed the walk to the Thorngate along the roads that were becoming more familiar to him. At the reception desk, a helpful and efficient woman quickly signed him up to both the writing course and also membership of the Community Association. He noticed that the building was quite busy on this Monday morning - there were indeed a lot of people who were enjoying the opportunity to become involved with in the courses or clubs that interested them. In 2081, he reflected, people seemed less interested in participation in groups - they tended to pursue their hobbies and interests on a more individual level, pursuing for example personal training plans in gyms and sports centres.

He joined some people who were walking along to

the refreshment room. At the counter, he showed his membership card and bought a cup of tea and a packet of crisps - only 10p, to his amazement! - and sat at a table next to a group of four women. He soon learned that these ladies were members of the "Cake Decorating" club and he was impressed by their enthusiasm - their whole conversation was about the skills they were learning. At another table, six men and women from a "Learning French" course were having fun speaking to each other in the language they were studying.

Presently Lucas left the Thorngate and strolled along Bury Road in the direction of the town, deciding to have a look at what Stoke Road had to offer. As he passed the Bogue Hall and The Vine, he felt a surge of excitement at the thought that he would be visiting these places tonight. He went in to a nearby newsagent's and bought a daily paper and an interesting looking computer magazine. He spotted a little cafe and went inside to see what was on offer there for lunch.

It was a strange little place - surely, he thought, old-fashioned even in 1981. Rather faded half-curtains adorned the windows. Each table was covered with a red and white check tablecloth, upon each of which were vinegar, tomato and brown sauce bottles, and battered metal salt and pepper pots. The menu offered home-cooked meals mostly of the fried variety and Lucas eventually chose sausages, chips and beans accompanied by two slices of bread and butter. Unhealthy it might have been compared with the types of food Lucas usually ate in 2081, but he thoroughly enjoyed his meal in the warm surroundings. Afterwards,he drank a couple of cups of strong tea while he glanced through the computer magazine. He found it fascinating to read about the early computers with their - to him - simplistic technology. But he knew that it was thanks to these early pioneers working on what was then a new idea that much of the future would come to depend upon.

Back at the hotel, Lucas wrote up a few more notes and observations before having a light snack. Then he got ready for the evening at the operatic society, feeling both excited and nervous at the same time, as he realised that tonight his personal feelings would very likely replace any sense of objective detachment. Just like everyone else in the operatic group, he would be going down there to enjoy himself.

Chapter Sixteen

When Lucas reached the David Bogue Hall that evening, he found that there were special arrangements for the auditions for *H.M.S. Pinafore*. Those who were auditioning for parts in the show were sitting near the stage, while the rest of the members took seats further back. There was a table near the stage, at which sat Andrew, the musical director, Angela, the producer and two other men and one woman who had been invited along from other local operatic groups to form a judging panel. Promptly at half past seven Michael, the chairman of the society, introduced the panel and announced the order of performance for the auditionees.

One by one, the would-be principals went on stage, each singing the set audition songs and speaking some dialogue relevant to the part they wished to play. When it was Beth's turn to audition for the part of Josephine, Lucas watched appreciatively as she performed the song stylishly. Two other women, Patricia and a girl he had not met before called Louisa, were also auditioning for the same part. Lucas thought that they were both pretty good too - in fact, he was impressed with almost all the people who went up on the stage. The auditions took well over an hour and then the tea and coffee break was announced while the judging panel conferred to make their important decisions as to who would be performing the leading roles.

Lucas took his tea and joined the chattering group which included Beth. He was happy when she returned his conspiratorial smile. "Well done!" he said. "See you later in the pub!" she replied quickly, before turning to talk to a couple of other girls.

After about fifteen minutes, the musical director called for order and everyone sat down. "Ladies and gentlemen," he said, "first of all I'd like us all to thank the members of our panel for coming here tonight to assist with the important job of selecting the principals for our performance of *H.M.S. Pinafore* which of course will take place next May. I know that Angela and myself have been most impressed with the high standard of all of you who sang tonight."

He gave way to Angela. "I'd like to echo what Andrew has just said," she began, "and just before we announce who will be playing which part, I do understand that some of you will be disappointed, but we do hope that you'll still give us your best support in the chorus." There was a murmur of assent and Angela briskly read out the names of those who had been allocated the main parts. As these were announced, here and there amongst the members were various reactions - nods of agreement, frowns, smiles and some murmurings. Finally, to a smattering of applause, the evening's business was concluded. Lucas, along with many other no doubt, had found the proceedings quite tense but of course on a personal level he was really pleased that Beth had got the part she wished for.

He walked over to The Vine with Bob, Barry and Vernon,

all of whom had been successful in the auditions. Beth, Belinda and a couple of other women walked on a little way ahead. How would he be able to get Beth on her own so that they could arrange their proposed Thursday meeting, he wondered. Once inside the pub, he managed to indicate to Beth and Belinda that he would buy their drinks, and was pleased to see that when he returned with their glasses they had managed to secure a seat for him.

Naturally, most of the conversation centred round the auditions. Bob proclaimed that the outcome had been pretty well as expected, but Barry disagreed with a couple of the choices. At one point, Patricia, who had been sitting at another table, came over and touched Beth on the shoulder.

"Well done," she said, before passing on to speak with Jacqueline. All this time, Lucas was wondering how he could manage to have a secret word with Beth - was their Thursday date still on?

It was time for another round of drinks. Lucas gathered up Beth and Belinda's glasses and prepared to go up to the bar, while the two women insisted on giving him the money. As Lucas approached the bar with Bob and Vernon, Beth walked past them.

"Nature calls," she said, giving him a quick glance. Hastily, Lucas put the empty glasses down on the counter and, seeing that the other two men were trying to attract the barman's attention, stepped outside into the corridor.

"Beth! Are we still on for Thursday?" he queried breathlessly. "Meet me at the Bun Penny in Lee at 7.45!" she said quickly. Lucas nodded and started to speak, but she interrupted him. "No more, now, see you there on Thursday!" she said and then she was gone. In a daze of happiness, Lucas stumbled back inside the bar and for once he didn't mind waiting to be served.

He took the drinks back to the table. "You took your time!" cried Belinda. While he had been at the bar, Angela, the producer, had joined their table and was already giving some indications to all those who had parts as to how she expected them to interpret the characters.

She smiled at Lucas. "Pity you're only going to be in the chorus, Lucas!" she said brightly. "I think you could have been a principal." As Lucas blushed modestly, Barry broke in with a laugh. "What, him?" he cried. "He's rubbish! Don't worry, Angela, we'll help him along in the chorus!" And they all laughed while Lucas felt happy for he knew that he had been fully accepted into this vibrant group of people.

Beth and Belinda were having a quiet conversation between themselves. Dennis came over to the table and asked the others what they thought about a new suggestion that had been put to the committee. A small professional recording company had offered to make a video of the society's performance of *H.M.S. Pinafore* when the show took place next year.

"Interesting," said Barry. "I think it would be a good thing to do, but it would be costly and not many in our group have got video recorders."

"How would it work?" asked Bob. "I believe they make a recording with a special camera and then they produce copies onto a tape," replied Dennis.

"H'mmmm," said Barry, "I know that Roy has a video recorder but he might be the only one in the group who has. I mean, I'd love to have one, because apparently you can record stuff off the television as well - but they are so expensive!"

While this discussion was taking place, Lucas was almost longing to tell them that in his time you could record and watch almost anything by way of your mobile phone for free! How everything had changed, he thought. Feeling mischievous, he said, "I'm going to make a prediction. One day in the future, I reckon they'll be able to invent some gadget like a little phone that you can carry around with you that takes pictures and films and does hundreds of other things!" They all laughed. "Lucas, you're the brainy one here!" said Bob, "so get going and invent one for us!" Ah, if only they knew, thought Lucas.

All too soon, it was time to leave the jolly atmosphere of the pub. As they went out, there were a few calls of "Good night! See you all next Monday!" "That's Thursday!" mouthed Lucas to Beth who nodded to him as she walked away to her car. It was a fine, clear night as Lucas walked happily back to The Alverbank. He looked up at the moon and stars, shining down on the world of 1981 just as they would a century later. An old saying came into his head - "The stars are the streetlights of eternity". And as he walked along passing the streetlights of a century ago he felt completely at home here in this time and, perhaps, more alive than at any time in his life.

Chapter Seventeen

Lucas slept well that night. Next morning, feeling refreshed, he was looking forward to his first visit to the Writers' Circle. It would provide another opportunity to observe and analyse social interaction at first hand. Carrying a small briefcase containing pens and a writing pad he walked along the streets that were now becoming familiar and arrived in good time for his course at the Community Association.

He consulted the large message board inside the entrance. This told him that his group was to meet in the Rogers Room, so he walked down one of the corridors to find the place. He went in and discovered two men and a woman already sitting there facing a large table. They nodded pleasantly to him, and after he had sat down, five more women and two men came in followed by a man of about Lucas's age. The latter proved to be the tutor, Ed Douglas.

Ed introduced Lucas to the rest of the group. "I'm sure you'll soon get to know everyone here," he said," and, Lucas, I wonder if you would care to say a few words about yourself by way of an introduction."

So Lucas explained briefly that he was visiting the area in order to do some writing for a social studies thesis from London University. "So, I do write, but not really in a creative way - it's mostly just factual - so I thought it would be very interesting to try and learn the techniques of how to write in a more personal way."

These words seemed to go down well with the rest of the group and Ed said, "Well, Lucas, welcome to our group. Now, how this course works: each week we discuss different ideas or themes, and then everyone produces some writing on the topic at hand. Then, if time allows, each person reads out his or her piece and we have a general discussion about each other's writing. After a few sessions, I'll be setting a title for a longer story for everyone to complete by the end of the term."

This was only the second week of the course. The first assignment had been for each group member to write a short piece about a favourite object in their home. One by one, they read out their essays.

"I'm afraid mine was very mundane," said one of the women after she had finished reading. "Not at all, Sheila!" said the tutor. "Remember, everyone sees and writes about things in dozens of different ways and we all learn a lot from hearing about other people's descriptions."

After they had all read their pieces, Ed talked about the way they might be improved upon, whilst at the same time bestowing plenty of praise for their efforts. Lucas was rather impressed with the tutor's skill in representing the results in a positive way.

Ed now announced that there would be a fifteen minute tea break and they all strolled along to the refreshment room at the front of the building. Lucas sat at a table with two of the younger women, Caroline and Liz, and an older man called Geoff. The latter told Lucas that he had recently retired from work in the Dockyard.

"I wanted to find something to occupy my mind," he said, "and, so far, I think this is a pretty good course." Caroline explained that she, like Lucas, was new to the area and wanted to do something interesting in between looking for a job. Liz told him that she was a part-time librarian and had joined the group in the hope of picking up some good ideas on how to write.

"My ambition is to write a great novel one day!" she said brightly. "I work surrounded by books in the library and I'd love to see my name on one of them in the future!"

Back in the Rogers Room, Ed Douglas announced the assignment for the rest of the session. "Now, everybody, have your pens and paper ready. You're all going to do what I call "Speedwriting." I shall give you a title and I want you to write about it in any way you wish for exactly fifteen minutes. All right?"

"Does it have to be a story?" asked Sheila. "No, it can be anything that comes into your head, fact, fiction, imagination, anything at all. Right - the topic is "November." Start writing - you have exactly fifteen minutes."

After some initial hesitation, the class began to write. Lucas decided to write down briefly what he had been doing since he arrived in Gosport in a very straightforward way, leaving out all the personal stuff. He hadn't finished when Ed told them that a quarter of an hour had passed and asked them to put down their pens.

"Now," he said, "I'd like to hear some of your efforts, and then we can have a general discussion about how you've approached this topic. Who'd like to go first?"

One of the older ladies raised her hand. "Mary! Good! Let's hear your piece."

She cleared her throat, stood up and began to read. "November. This month gives me mixed feelings. We have Bonfire Night and Remembrance Sunday, and once the month is over we're getting close to Christmas. I like walking at this time of year and then coming back to a warm home. On the other hand, we have some very cold days and there are no flowers and the trees are bare, and the darkness falls earlier and earlier. The best thing about November is that it is the birthday month of my eldest son, who is now grown up with a family of his own."

Mary sat down to a murmur of appreciation from the others and Ed praised her efforts. Encouraged by this each of the other group members, including Lucas, read out their short pieces. Finally the tutor summarised their work.

"You see, people," he said, "there are so many different ways of writing about this, and indeed any other, topic. You have all done very well - and I mean that sincerely -and I hope it will give you the confidence to express your ideas freely. Well done! Now, I'm going to set you an assignment for you to complete before next week's meeting. I want you to choose a television programme to watch and then write some critical comments about it. It can be a favourite programme, or, if you like, one that you dislike. Keep your writing short and I shall look forward to seeing what you have done next Tuesday."

As the class dispersed, Ed called Lucas over and having asked if he had enjoyed his first time in the group, handed him a list of the names of all the other members. Lucas adjourned to the refreshment room for a cup of tea, and read down the list of names. Among them of course were the three he had sat with during the break - Geoff Watkins, Caroline Shaw and Liz Howard-Benskin, the one who worked in the library and wanted to write a novel.

Liz Howard-Benskin. Lucas suddenly sat bolt upright. A strange realisation had come over him. In 2081, virtually anyone who had ever read a book knew the early twenty-first century works of one of the country's most loved and revered authors - Liz Howard-Benskin! So she would achieve her ambition. But of course he could not tell her so. How bizarre it all was, to know someone's future fate!

Chapter Eighteen

Lucas sat for some time, pondering the mysteries of travelling in time. Eventually he decided to clear his thoughts by doing something completely practical. Ever since arriving in 1981, he had been thinking about buying a car to give him the convenience of easier travel. From the evening newspaper,he had noted down a couple of garages that sold cars in Brockhurst and Forton. This afternoon, he thought, he would visit these places and see what was available. Maybe he could even buy one today - he thought he probably had enough cash in his wallet for a deposit.

Having consulted his bus timetable, he walked along from the Community Association to the corner of Gordon Road and caught the No.6. In a very short time, he reached Forton Road and soon discovered the first garage. He stood in some amusement looking at what, to his eyes, appeared to be a collection of ancient vehicles on the forecourt. How long would it take him, he wondered, to learn how to manage one of these primitive looking cars? In his own time, like almost everyone else, he owned a self-driving car and seldom used the facility whereby he could take actual control of it - normally, he just set the computer that told the car where to go and sat back to relax.

As he was staring at the cars a salesman appeared at his side. Lucas explained that he was a rather reluctant driver and was looking for a reasonably safe car just to use for local travel. The salesman showed him a few vehicles and in the end Lucas decided to buy a six-year-old red Ford Fiesta priced at £400. Having explained that he hadn't driven for a long time, he asked if the garage could arrange to deliver the Fiesta to his hotel. This was acceptable, the salesman said, for a few pounds extra.

Soon Lucas was seated in the scruffy office as the salesman arranged the sale. What a slow and tedious process buying a second-hand car was in 1981, Lucas thought. A wordy and complicated sales sheet had to be signed, together with an equally ponderous insurance document.

"And how would you like to pay, sir?" asked the salesman, "by cheque, or perhaps you have one of these new-fangled credit cards?"

"No," said Lucas rather nervously, "I wonder if I could possibly pay by cash? I have enough with me for a deposit and can hand over the rest at any time." The salesman looked rather quizzically at Lucas.

"Cash? Well....I suppose that would be all right. It's unusual though these days! It's rather old-fashioned! But we must have a deposit - fifty pounds?" Gratefully Lucas took out his wallet and handed over ten £5 notes. Finally, it was agreed that the car would be delivered to The Alverbank on the following afternoon, when Lucas would have the remaining balance of the money ready to complete the sale.

At last the transaction was over and Lucas left the garage with some relief. Still, he had now got a car and it would be very interesting to learn how to drive it. As he waited for the bus to take him back to Stoke Road, he smiled to himself as he remembered the salesman's remark. "Old-fashioned" was he? If only the man knew.......

In Stoke Road, Lucas called at the newsagent to buy the local paper and also a couple of magazines - "Motor" and a news periodical called "Now!" which he thought might give him a little more insight into what was happening in this world of 1981. Back at the hotel, he spent a quiet evening reading. He found the motoring magazine particularly interesting and realised his was looking forward to being able to try out his new car tomorrow.

Chapter Nineteen

After breakfast on Wednesday, Lucas thought he would spend the morning visiting the nearby town of Fareham. He knew the place well, with its huge shopping and entertainment centre which dominated the centre of the old town. But as he stepped from the No 8 bus on arrival, he found the centre of Fareham much changed. There was a shopping precinct, but it only covered part of the northern side of the main street, while older buildings occupied most of the rest of the area; long-vanished, of course, by his own time. It was strange to enter the precinct - a different one to 2081, although it looked quite new on this November morning. Inside, there was quite a variety of shops and places to eat, and Lucas mingled happily with a large number of people who were no doubt happy to be walking around in the warmth. He took a seat at the Garden Cafe, drinking a decent cup of coffee and eating a piece of home-made lemon cake. He had decided to buy a little radio today, to give himself some alternative entertainment to the television in his hotel room.

Soon he was in Dixon's, looking at a vast array of electrical hardware. To his eye, it looked like a museum of early appliances. He noticed a large display area which stridently advertised "The Latest Sensation - The Sony Walkman!" One of the models for sale offered both a tape cassette and a radio, so he decided to buy one. Pleased with his new purchase, he left the precinct and walked along to Weston Hart, a shop he had noticed earlier, to buy some cassette tapes. These, he knew, were becoming very popular at this time as an alternative to vinyl records in the days before compact disks had appeared. Inside the shop, he pored over a large selection of tapes. Most of the names of bands, groups and soloists were unfamiliar to him. Eventually, he chose "Greatest Hits" by Queen - one group that had retained popularity in his own time - and, in order to have some variety, he picked a double album labelled "Super Hits 1 and 2" with pieces from several different bands. Another tape album caught his eye - *Time* by the Electric Light Orchestra. Thinking how appropriate this title was to his own situation, he added it to his small collection.

He had had a very successful morning so far. He walked along West Street enjoying window shopping. He spotted a corduroy jacket in Millett's, and thinking about looking smart for his date with Beth tomorrow evening he went in and bought a similar one together with a new shirt. At a newsagent's near the bus station he purchased a daily paper and some packets of salt and vinegar crisps -a snack he was growing fond of these days. He noticed the large display of cigarettes behind the counter, and feeling quite wicked, decided to buy a pack as he remembered that Beth enjoyed an occasional smoke. Now he just had time for a quick sandwich lunch back in the Garden Cafe, before catching the bus back to his hotel - he mustn't be late for the delivery of his new car.

Not long after he had arrived back at The Alverbank, looking out of the window of the bar he saw his new car arriving. He hurried outside and after the mechanic who had brought the Fiesta along had handed him the keys, log book and manual in exchange for the rest of the money, he felt almost absurdly elated.

"Good luck, mate," said the mechanic, "they told me you haven't driven much lately, so I'm going back on the bus. Any problems, just give us a ring at the garage."

After the man had left, Lucas sat inside the Fiesta, studying all the knobs and dials on the dashboard and comparing them with the handbook. It all looked quite complicated, but he supposed he would get used to this vintage vehicle. As the hotel car park was empty, he thought he would try out his driving skills around the large open space. He was glad to see that the Fiesta had been equipped with seat belts - he remembered that these safety features were not compulsory just yet. He started up the engine, and drove jerkily around, finding it difficult to change the gears as he had never encountered a clutch system in his 2081 cars. At last he managed to complete a reasonably smooth circuit of the car park. For a moment or two, he wondered whether to try a short journey along the sea road beyond the little bridge, but decided that enough was enough for today. Dusk was falling and he sat in the safety of the car park, trying out the lights and indicators before locking up the Fiesta with a key in the old-fashioned way.

After dinner, he spent quite a lot of time in his room using his other new purchase, the Walkman. Considering the antiquity of the little device, he supposed that the sound quality through the headphones wasn't too bad, although far removed from the style of reproduction he was used to in 2081. He played some of the music from each of his new tapes, finding the *Time* songs particularly interesting. The lyrics of *Time*, sung by Jeff Lynne, were, he thought, surprisingly relevant to his own existence here in 1981. The album had a retro-futurist concept, as it featured a man living in 2095 describing the imagined technologies of that period while reflecting sadly on his vanished past. How strange that he had chosen this particular album, since he was indeed, as one of the tracks was titled, a 21st *Century Man*! When the tape had finished, Lucas sat quietly for a while. When, one day, he would return to 2081, he knew that he too, like Jeff Lynne, would truly "remember the good old 1980s."

Chapter Twenty

Lucas awoke on Thursday morning feeling less refreshed than usual. He was both excited but apprehensive about tonight's date with Beth. What should he do to pass the time before the evening? He had already decided that he couldn't yet risk driving his new car to the pub, so the first task was to organise a taxi for the trip. After the usual complicated rigmarole with the public telephone, he finally managed to book one for 7.15.

He spent the rest of the morning practising driving the Fiesta. After a couple of turns around the car park, he felt brave enough to venture out over the bridge on to the road alongside the bay. It was not busy on this November morning and he drove slowly and very carefully a little way along the road until he reached the large car park by the beach. He returned along the same road, turning the car round in a large open space at the other end of the bay before repeating the trip twice more. It was almost lunchtime now, and he felt much more competent in charge of this ancient vehicle.

Feeling pleased with himself, Lucas enjoyed his lunch in the hotel's dining room. Afterwards he tried to relax, listening to his new tapes on the Walkman and then reading a little. Feeling rather guilty and daring, he decided to try a cigarette. After all, he thought, people in 1981 obviously enjoyed smoking. And even though the habit had been banned in 2081, it was a well-known fact that there were still some small groups of rebellious folks who smoked in secret. After a few experimental puffs, however, he ground out the cigarette into an ashtray. Perhaps it took quite a long time for smoking to become enjoyable!

At five o'clock Lucas summoned up a couple of sandwiches from the kitchen and ate them together with a packet of his favourite crisps and a couple of cups of strong tea. He wondered about what might happen tonight. What would they talk about? Would Beth find him boring? After all, he could hardly say much, if anything, about his past life. One thing he was sure about though was that he wanted to know all about this interesting and attractive woman.

He bathed and dressed carefully, checking his image in the long mirror in the room more than once. He hoped that his attire, so odd compared with what he would wear in his own time, would appear reasonably fashionable. He started fretting again. What if his taxi was late? Or didn't even turn up? In either of these circumstances in his own time he could easily contact his date, but of course in 1981 this would not be possible. He needn't have worried, though. The taxi arrived at 7.15 on the dot and soon he was being whisked along the road to Lee and the Bun Penny.

Chapter Twenty-one

Here he was in the pub's car park and it was only 7.25. He was early, and he paced to and fro between the cars, partly to keep warm but mostly to try to calm his nerves. Just before a quarter to eight he was delighted to see Beth's white Austin 1100 drive in to the car park. He hurried over and opened her driver's door. They grinned at each other.

"Beth! It's lovely to see you," he cried, "you look great - I like your fur coat!" "Thank you, kind sir," she laughed, "let's get inside, it's freezing!"

He held the door open for her and they stepped inside the warm pub. They chose a small table quite near the bar itself. Beth asked for a schooner of sherry and Lucas stepped over to the bar. While he was waiting to be served, he looked around the pub. In 2081, he had occasionally been here, although the very old building had been turned into a "Victorian Theme" place, rather unsuccessfully he had always thought. He thought it looked much better at this time in the relatively simplistic decor, which more modestly suggested the Bun Penny's age.

When he brought their drinks back, Beth gestured to him to sit opposite her. "I like to be able to look at whoever I've come here with," she said brightly.

"Well!" he said, raising his glass, "here's to us!" For a few moments, they smiled at each other in silence. Lucas thought she looked really rather gorgeous. She was wearing a low-cut black dress with a striking golden necklace and matching ear-rings.

"Beth, I am really honoured that you have come out to see me tonight," he began. Beth laughed. "Lucas! You are so formal! Relax!" And gradually, as the conversation began to flow, he began to feel more at ease.

Beth was soon talking about her home life. She spoke very frankly. Her husband, she told him, was a very good man, but she found him boring. She wanted her life to be more exciting and to some extent the operatic group fulfilled some of her needs.

"And what about you?" she asked. "Have you got a woman tucked away waiting for you in London?"

"Not any more," he said truthfully, explaining that he had had a long relationship that had recently come to an end.

They talked about the people in the operatic society. Beth asked him what he thought about some of the other women in the group.

"They're all right," he said, "but there's only one I really wanted to see - and here she is!"

"Flatterer!" she cried, "You hardly know me. Do you know, Lucas, there;s something quite mysterious about you....it's almost as if you're hiding something!"

"No, no!" he protested guiltily, "I'm just plain old me!"

"H'm," she said. "I think you come from the moon! And you're not used to taking ladies out - look, my glass is empty!" And as he jumped to his feet, starting to apologise, she placed her hand on his. "I'm sorry, Lucas - only kidding!"

As the evening progressed, Lucas began to relax at last. They had more glasses of the potent sherry - Lucas noted that Beth insisted on paying her way. She accepted a cigarette from him and he had one too, this time finding it more to his taste. He realised that she was comfortable in his presence and quietly enjoying herself. She expressed herself so well, he thought, and in a voice that resonated in a rich,deep timbre. She began to tell him about how much she enjoyed singing and how she felt she came alive when she was on the stage in the shows.

"I hope you're going to enjoy being in "Pinafore", she said, "although didn't you say that you had joined so as to make some observations for your work?"

"Well, in the first place, that is true," Lucas replied, "but I didn't reckon on really having a personal involvement. Meeting you, I mean.....I have to say, Beth, I'm so glad we're sitting here together..."

She regarded him quizzically. Boldly, he went on, "What I'm trying to say, is that I think you and I could have a really great and unique relationship....." "Yes!" she interrupted, brightly, "Great and unique! I'm great, and you're unique!"

Lucas was amazed how quickly the evening passed. Beth looked at her watch and told him she ought to be on her way.

"It's twenty to eleven, and remember, I'm supposed to be at rehearsal," she said, "can I give you a lift back?"

"That would be great," he replied, "but I can ring from the bar for a taxi, I don't want to make you late."

"Nonsense!" she said briskly. "Of course I'll take you back. Just going to the ladies'."

While she was gone, Lucas tried to take in the surroundings of this cheerful pub. He had had a wonderful time - and he hoped Beth felt the same -and he wanted to etch the whole scene into his memory for ever. He knew he felt more alive here in 1981 than he had ever done in his own time - strange as this was, he knew it was true.

Beth emerged from the loo in a fresh waft of perfume. Tentatively, Lucas took her hand as they stumbled across to the car. Once inside, he was overcome with desire and soon they were cuddling and kissing. How good she tasted!

Then Beth emerged breathless from his embrace and gasped, "Stop it! Stop it, Lucas, oh, you're so sexy, this isn't right - but I love it!" And they hugged and kissed again before she finally pulled away. "Lucas, we must go!" Reluctantly, he sank back into the seat and soon she was driving, rather erratically, back to *The Alverbank.*

In the car park, they embraced once more. "Come up to my room," whispered Lucas. "I can't. No time. Must go now," she insisted. "Beth - when can we meet again? "he asked. "I don"t know yet- can't think straight just now - but it's been a fantastic evening - give me some time to work something out," she said breathlessly.

Lucas got out of the car and went round to the driver's side for one last kiss.

"Beth, you're just wonderful," he said, "I've an idea - how about we meet on Monday before rehearsal for a quick drink in The Vine?"

"OK!" she said, "Meet you at seven o'clock! Then we can decide what we're going to do next!" Lucas was delighted. "I'll see you there! Can't wait to see you again!"

She flashed him a quick smile. "Be off with you now. I've got to compose myself so I can get home safely!" And a moment later, she was driving away while Lucas waved until the white car was out of sight.

Lucas went to sit out in the garden under the stars, his brain spinning with emotion. He wished he could send Beth a message to tell her what a brilliant evening he had had. Eventually he retired to bed, quickly falling asleep and dreaming of Beth and the joys of this special evening.

Chapter Twenty-two

Lucas had not made any plans for Friday. It seemed a long time before he could see Beth again and he spent quite a long time after breakfast thinking about her and their special evening, but finally he settled down to make some notes for his project. When he had written down his objective accounts of the Writers' Circle and the operatic group, he decided to start a personal journal in which he could express his feelings about his experiences. He was pleased he had done this, realising just how strongly he felt for Beth. What had happened to him was so unexpected. It felt dangerous but thrilling at the same time.

In the afternoon he decided to take another short drive in his new car. Maybe, he thought, by Monday night he might feel confident enough to drive down to the opera group rehearsal. He took the Fiesta out along the bay road and eventually drove into Gosport. He was surprised to discover that he didn't have to pay to park in the large space behind the town shops - parking prices were astronomically high in 2081. He bought an evening paper,went into a little cafe for coffee and a piece of cake and had a short walk around the town, still fascinated to be among the people, sights and sounds of the twentieth century. By the time he returned to the car park, dusk was falling and he had to try out the Fiesta's lights for the first time as he drove back to the hotel. Accustomed as he was to the automatic lighting systems common to vehicles in his own time, he found the switching between sidelights, dipped headlights and full beam very confusing at first, What a variety of skills drivers of these days had to learn, he thought!

After dinner in the hotel, Lucas decided to work on his Writers' Circle assignment for the week. One of the television programmes on offer tonight was a quiz game called *Play Your Cards Right* and he switched on the set and settled down to make some notes. It was a lightweight and undemanding show, but he found it interesting. He was quite impressed with the host, Bruce Forsyth, who seemingly effortlessly held the show together while putting the various contestants at their ease. The format was quite simple, especially compared with the quiz and game shows he was used to in 2081, but it was very effective. When it was over half an hour later, he wrote down his views immediately. After he had read through his short essay, in which his comments had been largely positive, it occurred to him that here was another example of social interaction that he could include in his thesis, for there was an audience present at the show, which in turn was watched by many people in their own homes, thus presenting a two-tiered model of social interaction. Also, Lucas thought, watching television was a major pastime in 1981, but since there were only three channels to choose from, this more limited focus made it likely that people would discuss favourite programmes either within the family circle or the workplace or in other situations, thus providing further shared social interactions. How different from 2081 when everyone had their own particular playlists selected from the thousands of broadcasts on offer.

Chapter Twenty-three

Saturday dawned clear and bright. It was a good day, Lucas thought, to practice his driving skills. The roads were busier today, and he concentrated hard as he drove in and around Rowner and Bridgmary. He had a new experience - the fuel gauge indicated that the Fiesta needed filling up, so he stopped at the first petrol station he came across. In 2081, all cars were powered by electricity and merely needed charging from time to time but of course things were very different in 1981. Having watched some ancient films, Lucas had some idea of how refuelling worked. In reality, however, it was not an easy process. In the first place, he parked the Fiesta on the wrong side of the pumps. Having re-positioned the car, the next difficulty was that the pump was heavy and awkward to handle. He pressed the lever too feebly at first, then too heavily, splashing fuel over his shoes. All of this process was taking a long time, and he was flustered when an impatient motorist parked behind him hooted at him. At last he got the hang of it, finally managing to fill the tank - and just as he started the engine, he realised he hadn't paid for the petrol so he had to stop again and hurry inside the shop. Finally he drove away, feeling very annoyed with his incompetence and very conscious of the long line of cars that he had held up.

After this experience, Lucas felt in need of some relaxation. Driving back from Rowner towards Lee, it occurred to him to call at the Bun Penny for a coffee. "I'm becoming a romantic!" he thought to himself, as he realised that he was going there mainly to revisit the scene of his lovely evening with Beth. It was not yet lunch time, and the pub was quiet. He chose the same table where they had sat together on Thursday. Enjoying a pleasant cup of coffee, he mused on the nature of love and sexual attraction. He had been amazed at the powerful feelings that his experience with Beth had awakened. Somehow it had been different to any feelings he had known in his own time. Perhaps the technologies of 2081 - dating websites, dating at a distance, the fine tuning of one's personal predilections in a prospective partner, together with an extra sense of caution - had resulted in numbing natural desire to some extent. On the other hand, maybe his unique time travel experience was making him over-analyse his feelings. The truth was, he concluded, that there never had been and probably never would be a total solution to the mysteries of sexual attraction and loving relationships.

Lucas returned to The Alverbank and spent the afternoon trying out the different stations on his Walkman radio cassette. After he had read the local newspaper and glanced through his car magazine, he went downstairs to dinner. Tonight he was the only diner, and there was no-one else in the bar either. For once, he was feeling rather melancholy. He was missing the technologies and entertainment facilities and all the other facets of the life he had taken for granted in 2081. But after a couple of drinks he told himself to pull himself together. He was alive and part of the world of a century ago - a privilege that no-one had ever been granted. There was so much more to experience and enjoy. Henceforward his life pattern might be unscripted but the path would surely be stimulating and exciting.

Chapter Twenty-four

On Sunday morning, Lucas drove the Fiesta out to Bridgmary School to visit the Car Boot Sale he had seen advertised in the local paper. This type of buying and selling event was a new phenomenon in the early 1980s but in his own time it had ceased to exist. The ability to sell and buy various items via internet sites had superseded the old ways. People no longer had to go the trouble of transporting large numbers of items to a site before setting up tables and then standing around for hours hoping to make sales. But he was looking forward to seeing how the sales operated in 1981 and he knew he would be able to study a different type of social interaction at first hand.

Consulting his local map, he tried to memorise the route to the school grounds. Driving there carefully, he was quite surprised to see that many cars were heading for the same destination. Stewards directed drivers to parking spaces in the school grounds. The large concrete playground was already full and Lucas along with many others had to park on the playing field. It was a huge event. He walked along to the entrance and was amazed to see dozens of stalls and tables set out in front of the sellers' cars in long lines almost filling the large open grounds at the back of the school buildings. This was a popular way to spend Sunday mornings - Lucas had never seen so many people at a single event since he had come to the twentieth century.

He joined the large crowds of browsers looking at the tremendous variety of goods that were for sale at the individual tables. To his eyes, the event looked like one big sale of antiques. There were household wares, clothes, electrical items, lots of books and magazines, tapes and records, toys and games of all descriptions, ornaments and framed pictures. The sellers' tables were roughly arranged in long lines and Lucas walked up and down, trying not to miss anything. He paid a pound for a random collection of about twenty cassette tapes. At another table he sorted through a large selection of books, all priced at 5p. Most were contemporary paperback novels but he was interested to discover a hardback book called "The History of Gosport." Leafing through it, he decided it might come in useful for his research project. Certainly, he thought, it would be much more likely to contain facts about the town's past as opposed to the half-truths and general rubbish about Gosport that was often written about on the local websites in 2081.

"Only 5p?" he asked the smiling lady behind the table, holding up the book. "Yes!" she replied brightly, "but you can have another dozen for 50p if you like!"

"No, this one will be just fine!" he replied, "and please take 50p - it's well worth it!"

"Well, thank you kind sir! I wish all my customers were like you," she smiled as he handed over the coin.

After looking around for a while, Lucas joined many of the other shoppers inside the large school canteen where refreshments were available. He sat at one of the tables with a welcome cup of tea and a little packet of biscuits. Looking around the room at the other people, many of whom had bags bulging with purchases, he reflected on the popularity of this boot sale. It was very different from buying things from shops. Prices were certainly cheap and there was always a possibility that one might discover something of unexpected interest and there was plenty of cheerful banter between the sellers and buyers. All in all, he concluded, the boot sale was a positive and dynamic example of late twentieth century social interaction.

Back at The Alverbank, he had lunch in the dining room, which was quite busy today. His thoughts turned to the immediate future. He had been staying here for a fortnight now, and soon he must find somewhere else to live. Thanks to his original grant, he still had plenty of money left. He felt he would like to be more self-sufficient, so perhaps it was time to look for a furnished flat for the remainder of his time in 1981. He could visit some of the estate agents tomorrow.

In the afternoon, he amused himself by listening to some of the tapes he had bought at the boot sale. These were a real mixture. There were two or three featuring groups that he had never heard of, as well as a couple which had obviously been recorded from radio programmes, while he was quite impressed to listen to a tape full of stories and local information which was the work of a charity for the blind. Later, he switched on the television set and watched the erudite quiz game, "Mastermind" which was followed by a detective story called "Bergerac." He found he was enjoying these popular Sunday shows - perhaps, he thought, he was becoming a genuine twentieth century man! The next offering on the schedule was an episode of the American series, "Dallas." He had heard a couple of people at the operatic society discussing this show and he gathered that it was one of the most popular television series ever, watched by millions every Sunday. He watched the whole episode but could not see what all the fuss was about, although admittedly the plot and characters were completely unknown to him. To his eyes, the characters were obvious stereotypes, the storyline ludicrous and unbelievable. Perhaps the show's popularity was partly due to the lack of variety in television programmes at this time? Or was he perhaps just being pompous about it? After all, there were plenty of bad melodramas being shown among the thousands of channels available in 2081, but at least there was more opportunity to discover a programme that suited any individual taste.

He was much more impressed by a programme that followed the short news bulletin called "Genesis Fights Back." This was a discussion between people who had different views about the creation of the universe - those who favoured the Biblical version and those who believed in the Darwinian theory of evolution. Lucas found it to be very informative and balanced, full of reasoned and intelligent arguments - a type of programme, he thought, that was unfortunately uncommon in his own time. In 2081, incidentally, this long-discussed matter was no nearer to being solved.

Chapter Twenty-five

Next morning Lucas drove into Gosport, parked the car and went to visit three estate agents in the town. He emerged with some sheets containing details and photographs of various one-bedroom flats available for rent. Over a coffee in a pleasant little cafe called "The Black Cat" next to the National Provincial Bank, he studied the sheets. It took him a long time, but at last he managed to reduce the choice to just three properties - one flat in the town centre itself above a clothes shop, another in Stoke Road and a third above the Post Office in Lee. He went back to the estate agent's and to his surprise, the young salesman who he'd discussed his needs earlier offered to show him all three properties there and then. What a good service, thought Lucas, as they walked down the High Street to view the first flat. It was quite a good size, decently furnished and seemed to have been well looked after. But Lucas was very conscious of the constant noise of traffic outside, especially as he had become accustomed to the quietness of his room at the hotel.

The estate agent drove them to the next property in a street alongside Stoke Road. This one was on the second floor of an old house that had been converted into several flats. Although in a quieter situation, this one was smaller and rather gloomy and Lucas could not really imagine himself living there. While they were on their way to Lee to look at the next flat, Lucas had to remind himself that he could hardly expect any of the properties in 1981 to have any of the conveniences or style of the time he had come from. And fortunately, it was third time lucky as he looked around the large flat above the Post Office. It was bright, airy and (at least for these ancient times) equipped with modern fittings What was more, the back of the building provided a private parking space and also the road outside was relatively quiet. He made up his mind quickly and told the salesman he would like to rent the flat for six months. It was arranged that he should return to the estate agent's later in the afternoon when he could sign all the necessary documents.

After the man had dropped him back in the town, Lucas had lunch in the Wimpy Bar and studied the details of his new flat once again, feeling excited about having a place of his own. Back at the estate agent's. he went through the long process of signing various forms, paying a month's rent in advance. It was agreed that he could move in in two weeks' time.

Chapter Twenty-six

Back at The Alverbank, Lucas had time for a sandwich from the bar before getting ready to meet Beth at seven o'clock. He reflected on the long-winded process of securing a flat - in 2081, apart from looking over a place, or even taking advantage of a "virtual tour" of a property, the rest of the transaction would have taken mere minutes via the internet. He had been so busy today that he hadn't had time to become nervous about meeting Beth before the rehearsal.

He arrived five minutes early, parking the Fiesta in the little road across from the Bogue Hall, Promptly at seven o'clock, Beth drew up behind him in her 1100. He hurried over to greet her, feeling slightly nervous.

"Come on Lucas, let's get over to the pub. It's soooo cold tonight!" she said, and they hurried along to the Vine. At this time of night, the pub was empty and Lucas quickly brought their sherries over to a small table where Beth was taking off her light-coloured fur coat. Lucas felt relieved when she smiled her thanks - he had been worried because she had said little while they were hurrying to the pub.

"It's so good to see you again, Beth," he said, "and it's nice to meet you early."

"Well," she replied, "I thought it would be a good chance

to talk about you and I and....well, what we should do.... about our situation?"

For a moment, Lucas didn't quite know what to say. Beth continued: "Last Thursday was great, but over the weekend I started to worry about us - I almost convinced myself that we shouldn't carry on any more."

Lucas didn't know what to say, startled as he was at Beth's directness. She held up her hand. "Don't worry, Lucas, it's not you - I just get really confused and conflicting thoughts sometimes," She took a sip of her drink. Then she smiled over to him and squeezed his hand. "But..... now I've seen you again, the nice feelings have come back again. So.....if you can put up with me, I'd like to go on seeing you!"

Lucas let out a deep breath. "Beth, I'd like nothing better!" he said, feeling relieved and excited at the same time. The tension had been broken and they discussed where to go for their next date. Beth said that she could pretend that there was an extra principals' rehearsal this coming Wednesday.

"Let's go to Wickham, to Knockers Wine Bar - it's a great place, have you been there?" Truthfully, Lucas admitted that he had not, but readily agreed to Beth's proposal.

"Meet you in the car park, in the main square, 7.45 on Wednesday," she said decisively. "But look, we'd better get along to rehearsal now!" They finished their drinks quickly, left the Vine and were soon mingling with the group members on their way into the hall.

Inside Beth joined the other sopranos in the front row while Lucas sat with the basses at the back. Tonight was a "music only" rehearsal. Andrew, the musical director, announced that tonight they would try a complete sing-through of *H.M.S. Pinafore*. At first, Lucas found it hard to concentrate on the singing, his thoughts still centred on his encounter with Beth. Soon, however, the rehearsal was in full swing and it was obvious that everyone there was enjoying the special feeling of togetherness as they combined their voices. Lucas began to find it all quite exhilarating and when the rehearsal came to an end he felt thrilled to be participating in the communal social pleasure that this group had to offer.

Soon he was on his way to the Vine with the usual gang. It was slightly strange to be back in the pub where he had already been this evening but this time he was sitting with Bob, Barry and Vernon, facing Beth, Belinda, Patricia and Mary. He noticed tonight that Beth and Belinda seemed to be particularly close and he wondered if Beth had told her friend about what was happening. He was finding it quite hard not to keep looking across at Beth, but earlier when they had been alone she had asked him not to draw attention to their relationship when they were with the others.

As it happened, he spent most of the rest of the evening talking with the men. He talked about his new car and after this, he announced that he had found a flat.

Overhearing this, Belinda remarked brightly, "A flat? Wow. You'll be able to entertain all your women there!"

"Lucky bugger!" cried Barry, "fancy being single and carefree!" "Yes,all the rest of us are old married men," laughed Bob. "Tell you what, get some extra keys cut and then we can all use your new place from time to time!" As they all laughed and the friendly banter continued, Lucas felt happy that he had been fully accepted as a member of this friendly group.

As they left the pub, Lucas hoped he might be able to have some more private time with Beth before they went home. But tonight he was forestalled. Bob and Barry wanted to have a look at his new car, and he realised that Beth could hardly hang around to wait as it would seem rather suspicious. Never mind, he thought to himself as Beth waved as she drove away, we'll be having a whole evening to ourselves on Wednesday! He drove back to The Alverbank and sat happily in his room. It had been a stimulating evening. It was good to be alive in the winter of 1981!

Chapter Twenty-seven

After breakfast on Tuesday morning, Lucas drove the Fiesta down to the Thorngate Halls, looking forward to his second session with the Writers' Circle. When all the members of the group were seated in the Rogers Room, Ed Douglas began the meeting by asking each of them to read their television shows criticisms. Among the programmes chosen by the students, like Lucas, Geoff had watched *Play Your Cards Right*, while Sheila, the young housewife, and an older man called Tom had both chosen to write about *Dallas*. After Lucas had read out his piece, he felt that what he had written seemed rather commonplace and a trifle dull - Geoff's criticism of the same show had been, he thought, somewhat more scathing - but it was well enough received by the others. Lucas listened with particular interest to the two essays about "Dallas," having of course watched it himself. Both Sheila and Tom had obviously enjoyed the serial - Sheila confessed that she was an avid fan.

After the readings were complete, Ed threw open the floor for general discussion about the different criticisms.

"Come on, everyone," he said, "each and every one of your views is important! There is no right or wrong here, but we can all agree to disagree!"

At one point, Lucas brought forth his strong criticisms of "Dallas." He was a little worried after he had spoken in case he sounded too snobbish, but was pleasantly surprised when Sheila said she was impressed with the way he had deconstructed Dallas, even thought it was her favourite show.

"Lucas, your views come over as really fresh and interesting, even though I disagree with you," she said, "it's almost as if you had never even heard of the serial, let alone watched it before!"

When the general discussion finished, Ed said that he was pleased with their efforts, and made some points concerning the use of vocabulary and variety of style. After the tea break, Ed handed each of them a different picture that he had cut out from magazines and asked them to spend ten minutes writing about what they could see. Lucas' picture showed a man sitting in a library poring over a large book. After some hesitation, he let his imagination roam and started writing. He wrote about how people tried to find information and posed the question as to whether or not there were any limits to knowledge. He was quite pleased with this little philosophical effort. When the time was up, each student read out their short pieces. Lucas was of course particularly interested to hear Liz, who was to become such a famous author, read out her piece of writing which was a beautiful description of a quiet winter street under the moonlight.

Towards the end of the session Ed told the group that their next home assignment would be to write a short story. This was to be handed in on the last Tuesday of term, December 22nd.

"I shall read your stories over the Christmas break, and then spend the first session in the New Year discussing your efforts individually. Now, the subject - I want you to try to compose a short science fiction story!"

There were one or two doubtful looks around the room but Ed continued: "Now, I realise this might not seem to everyone's taste at first sight - but I trust you will all use your imagination and I am confident each of you will be able to produce a good tale. So that's all for today - see you all next Tuesday! And I will be happy to discuss your ideas next week, individually, for your proposed stories."

As they packed up and began to leave the room, Ed briefly intercepted Lucas by the door. "You know, Lucas," he said slowly, "something tells me that your science fiction story will probably involve time travel...." And he looked directly at Lucas for a moment. Then he shook his head. "Sorry. Don't mean to presume. Just had a strong feeling there for a minute!" And he left the room, leaving Lucas wondering about this latest example of a link between now and the future.

Chapter Twenty-eight

Over his lunch in the Stoke Road cafe, Lucas pondered on this last encounter. Thinking about it, however, was not going to solve anything, he decided. Instead he turned his mind on to more practical matters. He decided to take a drive out to Wickham - he thought it would be a good idea to check out the route to the village where he was to meet Beth tomorrow night. In 2081, he had been to Wickham once or twice - it was a specially designated "preserved village of special interest," and was a popular tourist attraction, affording as it did a quaint and fascinating alternative to the bland urbanised conurbations which surrounded it. Getting there in 1981 however was not particularly easy, accustomed as he was in 2081 to sitting comfortably in an automatic driverless vehicle which transported him along a straight highway from Fareham. This afternoon he found himself driving rather nervously along a difficult stretch of road after negotiating the exit northwards from Fareham. How careful and alert he had to be while driving in this unfamiliar environment! Nor was he impressed by the local driving standards. No wonder there had been so many accidents in these olden days, he thought grimly.

At last he arrived in Wickham and having parked in the Square looked around for the wine bar where he was to meet Beth tomorrow evening. He soon spotted "Knockers." It was an ancient-looking but pleasing timber-framed building. He went inside and discovered a large brick-lined room with wooden beams in the ceiling. There were some small private booths along a couple of the walls. At the bar, he ordered a cup of coffee and took it over to one of the little booths. While he drank it, he thought about the science fiction assignment. Should he attempt a made-up story? Or should he perhaps write a truthful account of his real travel through time? Once more, he thought about Ed's reaction this morning, and the similar incident with the vicar the previous week. They seemed to have perceived something odd about him. Did Beth have any inkling that he was different in some way? Did anyone else that he had met?

Eventually Lucas left the bar and drove back through Fareham to The Alverbank. The roads were busy and he was glad he had explored the route in advance of his meeting with Beth on the following evening. Once again, it was a quiet night at the hotel. After dinner, he sat in the bar reading the local history book he had bought at the Boot Sale. Interestingly, there was a little bit about the history of The Alverbank. He learned that the building had been put up in the 1840s as a large house for a novelist and journalist called John Wilson Croker, a well-known local figure at this time. Many celebrities of the period had visited and stayed there over the next few years, including Queen Victoria's second son, Prince Alfred. The Alverbank had passed into the hands of various families before eventually becoming a hotel. So, Lucas mused, even in 1981 it was already well over a hundred years old, and it was still standing in his own time. His thoughts roamed over the passage of time. Somehow, he reflected, it did not seem fair that buildings could survive for so much longer after the people who had filled them with life had passed on. And most of the elderly folk who lived in The Alverbank and the surrounding community in 2081 were just babies or infants at this moment that he was sitting here in the bar. Another sobering thought was that not one of the new friends he had met on his travel to this time would be around to see the future that he knew so well.

But Lucas knew there was no point pursuing these depressing lines of thought for too long. There was absolutely nothing he could do to change things. He was also aware that gloomy philosophising would be the last thing on his mind when he was enjoying a delightful time with Beth tomorrow evening. After all, each and every person that had once been in this old place would have experienced all the emotions that life has to offer. Another thought struck him - he had been able to travel back to 1981; maybe some day he could go back to Gosport in the nineteenth century and actually meet the ghosts of The Alverbank in living form!

Chapter Twenty-nine

Perhaps rather surprisingly, Lucas slept very well that night and awoke feeling refreshed and full of energy. Naturally, his first thoughts were of the evening which lay ahead, but he decided he must make the most of the hours before. He decided to visit the local library - he had enjoyed the Gosport history book and wanted to find out more about the place. He drove into town and was soon walking towards the library. It looked quite a new building, although different from the one he knew in 2081. Inside he found there were many differences to the library he was accustomed to. The lending section consisted entirely of books, rows and rows of them. Of course, there were facilities for individual study, reference books, maps, old photographs and little microfiche machines to use for reading old newspapers and documents. But it was such a contrast to the libraries of his own time. In 2081 these had become "Discovery Centres," containing every type of electronic media as well as providing on-line courses, space for community meetings, entertainment and even cafés. Worthy as the 2081 libraries were, Lucas found the quieter 1981 version rather pleasing and comfortable.

He went downstairs to the reception area, intending to ask for assistance with local history. He was pleased to see Liz from his writer's group behind the desk - he remembered she had told him that she worked part-time in the library. They greeted each other warmly and after he had told her what he was looking for, she showed him where to find the necessary local materials. Armed with some local books and old photographs, Lucas sat in the reference section and spent the next half an hour making some notes on the history of Gosport.

Laying aside his pen, he thought that he would like to talk to this young woman who was to become such a famous author in the next century. He went back to the reception desk and smiled at Liz.

"I hope you won't think I'm being presumptuous," he said rather nervously, "but I wonder if you would possibly care to join me in a cup of coffee?"

"Why, thank you Lucas!" she replied brightly, looking at her wristwatch. "I have a break in ten minutes - I usually pop over to the Black Cat for a drink -shall we meet there?" "That will be just fine, Liz!" he smiled, and went back upstairs to put away the materials he had been using.

When he came back down, a different woman had taken Liz's place at the desk and she was waiting by the main doors. They walked quickly over to the cafe and were soon chatting amiably over cups of coffee. Naturally the conversation began with their experiences at the writing group.

"What about this science fiction story Ed has asked us to write?" said Liz. "I mean, I don't think I'll be able to come up with much for something like that. I'm not really into that sort of thing......" She paused and suddenly looked intently at Lucas before continuing, "but - somehow - I know you will write something really brilliant and unusual!"

He held her gaze and nodded agreement. "Lucas - I hope you won't mind me saying this - but there's something mysterious about you. I get this feeling that you have had - how shall I put it? - some really special experiences....." Then she tossed her head and laughed. "Sorry! Just babbling as usual! Pay no attention!"

"Not at all Liz!" he said warmly, secretly fascinated that she had sensed something about his unique existence in this world. "I'll tell you more about myself another time," he said, "but just now I want to hear more about you. I know you want to become a famous author one day and I must say, that everything that I've heard you read out from the exercises in the Writers' Circle has been brilliant - and I'm convinced that one day you will achieve your ambition!"

"Flatterer!" she laughed. "But thank you. And what type of novel to you think I should write?"

"Ah, now, let me think!" said Lucas, sitting back with a smile. He could hardly tell her that she was destined to write a most popular series of novels, fifteen in all, about the adventures of a troubled doctor who dabbled in crime-solving. Her first book would be published in 1988 and her last, and most famous, after the great pandemic of 2020. But, feeling somewhat mischievous, he smiled across at her. "How about a detective series?" he suggested. "Although, there are quite of lot of those -

maybe you could have a different slant on the genre - oh, say, perhaps a medical man who solves mysteries in his spare time?"

Liz sat bold upright in her chair. "Lucas!" she cried. "You must be a mind-reader! Believe it or not, that is almost exactly one of the ideas I have been turning over in my head for quite a while now! Maybe this is a sign that I should really get down to writing properly!"

"You must!" said Lucas warmly "and I predict that you will eventually write a whole series of best-sellers!"

She studied him carefully. "It's almost as if you can see the future! I am so encouraged by what you have said. Recently I've been feeling as though my ambition to write is perhaps a waste of time,but now you've convinced me to carry on! Let's talk again - but now I must go back to work."

She stood up quickly and Lucas rose too. "No, stay and finish your coffee," she said, "I"l see you again at the group next week. She walked quickly to the door, stopped and came back again. "This has been such an exciting chat, Lucas - next time you must tell me about your science fiction ideas - I think you may well be very interested in time travel." And she touched his hand briefly and was gone.

Lucas stayed on in the cafe for quite some time, eventually ordering lunch. This had been a fascinating meeting. Liz had obviously sensed there was something strange about him. Just like the similar feeling that had struck the vicar and the writers' tutor, it seemed as though it was just a momentary flash of the strange truth concerning Lucas and his presence here in 1981. And here was another thing - had their conversation been instrumental in leading Liz Howard-Benskin on to the path towards the fame she would achieve in the future? When I get back to my own time, he thought, I shall look up everything I can find about her life and works. Maybe she might even have referred to this very meeting this morning.

Chapter Thirty

Back at The Alverbank in the afternoon, Lucas knew that he must put aside his philosophical musings for the time being. Tonight's encounter with Beth would be a very different kind of meeting, promising raw emotion and sexual excitement - at least, he hoped it would.

After a change of clothes, a bath and some careful grooming, he set out early for Wickham. Driving carefully along the dimly-lit roads, he pulled up in the centre of the Square with plenty of time to spare. He played his *Time* tape in the car as he waited nervously for Beth to appear. Promptly at 7.45 Beth drove her white 1100 into the space next to Lucas' car. He jumped out eagerly to greet her. How fine she looks, he thought, she brightens up the dark night with her presence. She was as excited as he was and they walked hand-in-hand into the welcoming warmth of the wine bar. It was quite busy, but they found one of the empty booths.

"Ah, this is good - nice and private!" exclaimed Beth. "Let's have a bottle of wine between us tonight, and then you needn't have to keep going up to the bar!" They looked at the wine list and Beth chose "Black Tower", a brand that Lucas had never heard of before. When he returned from the bar with this interesting-looking bottle, Beth had removed her little fur coat to reveal a low-cut white blouse over a brown skirt as she smilingly indicated for him to sit opposite. How gorgeous she looks, he thought, with her fashionably bouffant hair and striking eye make-up.

"Beth, you look wonderful!" he said. "Not so bad yourself - I like your suit!" she replied cheerily, and they laughed happily together.

The evening passed in a whirl of pleasure. Conversation flowed easily. Often they held hands across the table. It was one of those special evenings, Lucas thought, that should last for ever. But the time just flew by so quickly. All too soon, it seemed, the wine bottle was empty. Should they have another one? "Better not," said Beth, "much as I'd like to - let's have a coffee instead."

When Lucas came back from the bar with their coffees, Beth looked at her watch. "It's almost ten," she said, "and I must get back before half past eleven. Take me somewhere now!" He needed no persuasion. Soon they were hurrying out into the Square and Beth jumped in to the Fiesta. After a quick kiss and cuddle Lucas drove them to a quiet field alongside a small road a little way from the village centre. And there, on the back seat of the car, under the shelter of ancient trees, they made love just as so many had done since time began.

Afterwards they sat in a dishevelled heap in the back seat, locked together in warmth and sheer pleasure. Beth was the first to stir.

"That was so wonderful, Lucas," she breathed, "but we must get going now!" So he drove them carefully back into the Square, where they kissed and hugged again before Beth broke away.

"Must go now!" she said, stepping out and opening her own car's door. Lucas waited while she settled into the driving seat. "Am I presentable?" she laughed.

"Beth, you are fabulous and you can present yourself to me any time you like!" he replied. "Can we meet tomorrow night? How about in The Vine at ten, after your real rehearsal?"

"No, not there," said Beth, "it would look so obvious to all the others - I'll drive over to the Bun Penny after rehearsal and meet you there?" "Oh. Beth, I'll be there! But I don't want you to go tonight!"

"Nor me, but I must. Will you follow me into town and make sure I get there o.k.?"

After a final embrace, Lucas returned to the Fiesta and as Beth drove off, he pulled in behind. He forced himself to concentrate on driving, although his mind was all over the place. Soon they reached the town and once he saw that she was safely entering the little road where she lived, he carried on to The Alverbank. Before going in, he could not resist the urge to sit in the back seat where they had so recently made love. Just for a few moments, he breathed in the lingering smell of Beth's perfume. At last he went up to his room, and re-lived the wonderful moments of the evening before falling into a deep sleep.

Chapter Thirty-one

Next morning, all he wanted to do was to think about Beth and how much she meant to him. Was he in love with her? Or was it all sex? All he knew was that he wanted to be with her all the time, even though he knew this was just not possible. At least he could see her tonight, even if it was only for an hour or so. Eventually, his strong sense of self-discipline took over and he set aside his personal thoughts, albeit reluctantly, and spent most of the day organising his project work. In the early evening, he enjoyed another of the hotel's fine dinners - this was something, he realised, that he would miss when he had to cater for himself in his new flat!

Time seemed to pass very slowly. It was so exciting to be seeing Beth again so soon after last night's marvellous meeting. He pictured her performing her songs at the rehearsal and thought about how she was able to change roles. One minute she was quiet, unassuming and quite shy - the next she could turn into a super-sexual, impulsive lover.

Finally it was time to drive to the Bun Penny. He arrived in the car park at a quarter to ten, hoping that Beth's rehearsal hadn't finished early. But all was fine. Just before ten he saw her white car drive in and he jumped out at once to greet her. Beth returned his kiss quickly, then said, "Let's go in - I'm in need of a drink!"

Inside the pub, Beth asked for a schooner of sherry. Lucas had one too and soon they were sitting opposite each other. Beth took a large gulp of her drink.

"Oh, I needed that," she said "Andrew worked us really hard tonight." For the next few minutes, she talked about the rehearsal and Lucas found himself wishing he had been there to watch it all. Eventually Beth said, "You're rather quiet tonight, Lucas!" "Oh Beth, I can't stop thinking about last night! Wasn't it just wonderful! You made me so happy!"

To his dismay, Beth looked away from him and spoke quietly.

"Lucas, yes, it was a great evening. But...what are we going to do from now on? I've been thinking about our situation all day. Don't get me wrong - I was in a wild mood last night - it happens to me sometimes - oh, it's difficult to put it into words - oh, don't look so sad, Lucas!"

"But Beth!" he stammered, "we had such fun! We're really good together, I just feel so much for you!"

Beth held up her hand. "Lucas, I don't want you to fall in love with me. I am married, and I have no intention of leaving my husband. He might be boring, and I don't think he really fancies me, but he's a decent man." For moment, Lucas didn't know what to say, as he felt a rising sense of panic. How had the conversation turned this way?

But Beth carried on trying to explain how she felt.

"When I get this special mood - like I did last night - absolutely anything goes. But then when I feel sober I start worrying about the risks."

She sat back, looking away from him. He realised that it had been difficult for her to say these things and for a short while he was uncertain how to respond. Finally, he said, "Beth....I don't want our affair - our friendship - to just come to a stop like this."

Now she looked directly at him. "Nor do I, really," she murmured. "Lucas, I get in such a muddle sometimes. It's not your fault. And there's another thing - I feel I don't really know you, I mean, you're a very private person and you don't ever really talk about your life! And you're single, and one day you'll meet somebody else."

"Beth, there could be no-one to even compare to you!" he cried, and, then, seeing her frown, he gathered his thoughts together and spoke more calmly.

"Beth. Believe me, I do respect and understand your position. It is good that you've told me how you feel. Forgive me. I've been selfish. I should have thought about your life much more and I promise you I'll never try and force you into a corner."

She looked at him more cheerfully. "Lucas," she said, "let's just see how it goes? I really did have a wonderful time last night." And he felt better to hear her say that.

They talked some more. They both felt better to have cleared the air. At last they agreed that they both found each other stimulating and exciting. "Let's talk more, said Beth finally. "Meet me at seven before rehearsal again on Monday. And now, I must go - I'm always saying that!"

"Come and sit with me in the car for five minutes," he pleaded.

"Just five,then," agreed Beth. Once inside his car, the sensible, careful and sober words they had exchanged were quickly replaced by fierce and passionate kissing. Eventually she pulled away and hurried to her car, driving off quickly with a wave to Lucas as she left.

Back in his hotel room Lucas spent a lot of time thinking about what Beth had said. It was true that ever since he had fallen for her, he had been selfish in the way he had only considered his own feelings. He had not really looked beyond the image that Beth had presented to him as they had so obviously been attracted to each other. Really, he thought, he was glad she had explained so much about herself and her situation and he resolved to try to consider her feelings more sensitively in future. And after all, their last few moments tonight had shown that they both wanted to continue the thrill of their special relationship. He spent a little while wondering whether to phone her tomorrow, perhaps to apologise again for his selfishness, but on reflection he decided not to do this - it might seem that he was overdoing things again.

Chapter Thirty-two

Over the weekend, Lucas turned his attention to the impending move to his new flat. Enjoyable as his stay at The Alverbank had been, he was looking forward to having a place of his own. On Friday morning, he drove to Lee. It was cold in the flat, and he couldn't use the heating until Monday, so he sat in his overcoat and spent some time making notes on what he would need - bed linen, bathroom equipment, kitchen items and so on. The lounge chairs were comfortable enough but the room needed brightening up with cushions and new curtains. At least there was a telephone, and the kitchen had a fridge and an electric cooker as well as cups and saucers, plates, dishes, knives, forks and spoons. Obviously he would need to buy a lot of stuff - food of course, together with supplies of utilitarian but necessary things such as washing up liquid, cleaning materials and so on. It took a long time to make his lists and he must organise his buying to make it as easy as possible. He had, at least, been used to living in a place of his own in 2081; but when he had moved into his Gomer Lane house he had had the convenience of being able to order virtually everything, including groceries, via the internet. How much more difficult these things were in 1981!

He spent the rest of the day going to the shops in Gosport and Lee, returning more than once with bags full of stuff to store in the flat. In Radio Rentals, he bought a reasonably cheap television set, and also chose a hifi unit which could play tapes and records whilst also providing him with radio entertainment. Having stored these "luxury" items in the Fiesta's boot, he went along to the well-stocked second-hand record shop in Bemister's Lane and bought a few long-players for £1 each. When he had finally delivered all his purchases into the flat, he was exhausted. Gratefully he drove back to the hotel for dinner, reflecting ruefully on the practicalities of moving house.

On Saturday, Lucas drove to the new supermarket in Gosport in order to stock up with food. Any frozen or chilled items would have to wait till Monday, as he couldn't store them in the flat until the electricity was switched on. It was an interesting, if unfamiliar, experience for him as he negotiated his trolley around the aisles. He wasn't used to this at all. In his own time you selected what you needed from the shelves by pressing individual buttons and the items you had chosen appeared in bags at the checkout for you to carry away. After he had managed to load up the trolley and push it along its erratic wheels to the checkout, he finally emerged with bags full of provisions. He noted with some surprise just how much food was in plastic wrappings, for in 2081 this form of packaging had long been discontinued. He enjoyed a hearty lunch in the Wimpy which today was busy with families, Back at his flat, he put the food away in the kitchen cupboards. He was looking forward to moving in.

Sunday was his last day as a guest at The Alverbank. He spent time working on and arranging his notes for his thesis and then brought his personal diary up to date,

What a lot had happened in the short time he had been living in 1981! He collected up his belongings ready for the move tomorrow before going down to the dining room for dinner. Afterwards he sat in quiet contemplation in the bar. Of course it would be good to move into a place of his own, but he would always associate his time at the hotel with many special memories.

Chapter Thirty-three

Next morning he had breakfast for the last time in the hotel and went to the reception desk to pay his bill. He thanked the manager for his stay there, commenting particularly favourably on the excellent meals he had enjoyed. In return, the manager extended his best wishes for Lucas' future and remarked that he had been a model guest.

"You will always be welcome here, sir," he said, "and I hope you will drop in from time to time to see us!" The two shook hands and Lucas loaded up the car before driving off to the Gosport estate agents to complete the formalities of taking possession of the flat in Lee.

It was a bright, cold morning and presently he was inside the flat which looked bright and welcoming in the sunlight. He switched on the electricity, turned on the heaters and the fridge before walking out into Lee to have a cup of coffee at the Penguin cafe. He had been pleased to see that the little town had a Co-op, a Lipton's and a greengrocer's, so he would be able to buy milk, bread, margarine and all the other small items he needed in the flat. He enjoyed a bracing walk along the beach before visiting these shops, finally returning to the flat once again weighed down with heavy bags. Inside, the rooms had warmed up nicely and Lucas made himself a cup of tea and settled back into the comfortable armchair, feeling contented and rather proud of having a place to call his own. Of course, he was looking forward to the operatic rehearsal in the evening, and the prospect of seeing Beth again.

In the early evening, Lucas made his first meal since leaving 2081. He cooked some sausages and bacon, with some oven chips and baked beans. It was a simple enough dinner, but he was absurdly proud of his achievement and he reckoned it tasted pretty good. At last it was time to get ready for the evening rehearsal.

Chapter Thirty-four

Lucas drove along the main road towards Gosport and parked as usual in the side road near the David Bogue Hall just before seven o'clock, eagerly awaiting the arrival of Beth. As ever, she was right on time and soon they were sitting in The Vine with their drinks. Beth asked him all about his new flat.

"Come and see it tonight!" he offered. "No, not tonight," she said, "we must be careful - it would look rather suspicious if we both disappear straight after the rehearsal and it will be too late after pub time."

For a moment, Lucas felt disappointed, but then Beth had a better idea. "Look, on Thursday I must go to the principals' practice - but I believe I'm only going to be needed until half time this week. So......I could come to the flat then - it would be at about nine?"

"Oh, Beth, that would be great!" he enthused. " I'll have it all neat and tidy for you!" She laughed and said, "And make sure it's warm! Otherwise I'll leave straight away!"

It had been a very relaxed little meeting, and Lucas was buoyant as they left the pub to join the others on their way to the rehearsal hall. Inside, there was a pleasant bustle of anticipation as this was the first time they were to use the stage. Andrea, the producer, soon took charge. The men of the chorus went up onto the stage and she arranged them into small groups for the opening chorus of the show. She outlined the movements and business that she had planned out. Tonight, the chorus were still permitted to use their scores but she asked them all to try and learn the words of the opening number before next week. Angela put them through their paces for about half an hour while the ladies and the principals looked on. Lucas found himself enjoying the camaraderie of it all.

During the interval Lucas chatted to a few of the people he already knew, occasionally catching Beth's eye as she talked with a small group of women. The second half of the rehearsal consisted of the first reconstruction of the finale of Act One, which involved the whole chorus and most of the principals. Lucas noted that while allowing for some light-hearted banter and laughs among the chorus, both Andrea and Alan, the musical director, kept a firm hold on proceedings, and the group worked hard and responded well.

Just before ten o'clock, Andrea and Alan brought the practice to an end. "You've all worked very hard tonight," said Andrea. "Thank you all. Next Monday we shall go through those same pieces again, so please make an effort to learn both the words and music." As they prepared to leave, Lucas felt the shared enjoyment of the evening. They had indeed worked hard but it was good to be part of such a good team.

It was a cheery party that strolled along to The Vine. As was becoming customary, Lucas bought sherries for Beth and Belinda over to one of the tables. Tonight, besides the usual gang, there were two or three other members of the group whom Lucas did not know. One of them, Calvin, who was to play the part of the leading man, Ralph Rackstraw, sat next to Beth. While Lucas was talking about his new flat to Bob and Barry, he couldn't help but notice that Calvin seemed to be paying a lot of attention to Beth. Quite irrationally, he felt a touch of irritation. He quickly told himself that he must not allow himself any feelings of jealousy - it was silly and unnecessary, and after all Beth had told him to be careful not to "fall in love" with her.

Just then, Vernon, who had been over at another table, came over to Lucas. "Hey, mate," he said, "are you doing anything this Saturday night? Because we're having a gathering at our place, a little pre-Christmas party - we'd be glad if you'd like to come!"

Lucas was delighted and accepted the invitation at once. "Great!" said Vernon. "You'll know quite a few people there - some of the opera crowd are coming along. Here, you don't know where we live - it's on Privett Road - I'll just write down the address. O.K. then, come any time after eight. Bring a bottle and we'll provide a few snacks. Look forward to seeing you!"

And Vernon went off to ask the others round the table. Lucas was pleased and excited to have been asked. Here was another opportunity to observe 1980s social interaction of a different kind; and even better to participate in it. He noted with pleasure that Beth had also accepted the invitation.

After Vernon had moved away to another table to invite

some others, Belinda grinned across the table at Lucas. "Glad you're coming to Vernon's do! His parties are legendary - lots of food and drink and dirty dancing in dark rooms!" Lucas laughed.

"Sounds intriguing!" he said. Indeed it was, he thought to himself. It seemed as though parties in this time might be considerably more sensuous than the rather antiseptic ones he was accustomed to in 2081.

The conversation at Lucas' table turned to the topic of television programmes. Roy, having recently visited the United States on a business trip, talked about the phenomenon of cable television which was popular across the Atlantic.

"There are just so many channels to choose from over there," he said, "I reckon it'll be the way forward over here eventually." Some of the others chose to disagree with Roy's prediction but Lucas could not help suggesting that in twenty years time there would be hundreds of television channels available, beamed down from satellites. Barry was scornful.

"Never, Lucas! Interesting idea though. But we'll be lucky to even get this new Channel Four effort to see."

This light-hearted chatter led on to some discussions about the future in general, Lucas listened in fascination as the others talked about the possibilities of flying cars. households served by robots, interplanetary travel and other ideas. He joined in, supporting the predictions that he, of course, knew would come to pass.

"I'm impressed with your knowledge, Lucas!" cried Bob. "You're very convincing - I reckon he's come back to us from the future!" And while Lucas joined in with the laughter at this remark, he felt a frisson of strangeness. If only they knew!

At closing time, as they walked back from the pub Lucas was able to keep close to Beth. Tonight Belinda had parked her car elsewhere so Lucas and Beth were able to sit together for a few moments in the Fiesta. After some exciting kissing and cuddling Beth left for her own car and Lucas drove back to his new flat, happy in the knowledge that she would be coming to visit him on Thursday. He had left the storage heaters on while he was out, so the flat was warm and welcoming. He made himself a hot chocolate drink and took it over to sit in the chair beneath the long window. For a while he kept the curtains open and surveyed the quiet street beneath. It had been a good evening, he reflected, and at last he was living in a place he could call his own.

Chapter Thirty-five

After a decent night's sleep, Lucas awoke quite early to the unfamiliar sounds of traffic outside. Looking outside, he observed that Lee was coming to life on this chilly December morning. Quickly switching on the heating, he made himself a rather rudimentary breakfast of cereal and toast - not exactly up to the standard of The Alverbank's food, but it would suffice for now.

Before setting off for his Writers' Circle group, he went down the stairs and into the Post Office below. He introduced himself to the shop keeper, who pleasantly expressed the hope that Lucas would be happy living in the flat above. Lucas bought a morning paper and a couple of interesting-looking chocolate bars before going out to the car park at the back to start up the Fiesta. The side roads were icy and Lucas was relieved to find that at least the main roads leading into Gosport had been gritted. He arrived at the Thorngate in plenty of time for his writing group.

As usual, the members were gathered in the Rogers Room and Lucas was pleased to see that Liz welcomed him with a wave and a warm smile. Today, Ed set them their first task which was to write for about twenty minutes about any particular childhood memories, which he would get them to read out later. Lucas had to ensure that he did not write down any anachronisms.

After a little thought, he decided to write about a somewhat painful memory. When he was eight or nine, his parents had spent a weekend away in London (they were visiting the centenary celebrations to mark the opening of the Planetarium, but of course he could not mention that!) and he had had to stay in Gosport at his aunt's house. He had desperately wanted to go on the trip. Then on the following Monday morning at school, his teacher had asked if anyone had done anything especially interesting over the weekend. Keen to make an impression, Lucas had claimed he had been to London, embellishing his tale with imaginary details of the sights he had seen. His teacher had been pleased, he remembered, but it all went wrong when another of his classmates called Tony put up his hand and said that he had seen Lucas in Lee with his aunt on the Saturday afternoon! As Lucas wrote all this down, the memory of his embarrassment in front of the whole class, and the consequences of his lie - a sharp note to take home to his parents - was still quite unpleasant.

When they had all finished their accounts, there was time for half the class to read out their stories before the break. In the refreshment room Lucas sat next to Liz and while the others at his table were discussing their stories, they were able to have a short private chat.

"Lucas, I want to thank you for taking so much interest in my dreams to become a writer," she said warmly. "I've even made some notes and outline a story on the lines you suggested!"

"I'm glad I was some help. Liz!" he smiled. "I'd really like to see what you have written so far - and have you started your science-fiction story yet?"

"I have," she said, "I'm quite pleased with it so far.....I say, why don't we meet tomorrow again, like we did last week in my break, and then we could show each other what we've written so far?" Lucas was very happy to agree to Liz's proposal. Another interesting encounter to look forward to!

After the break, the rest of the group, including Lucas, read out their accounts of childhood memories. All were very different in style and character and for the rest of the session Ed the tutor led a lively discussion on the content and styles of the various stories. Just before the end, the two older women, Mary and Catherine, had an announcement to make.

"As we're getting close to the end of term," said Mary, "Catherine and I were wondering if we might all get together after our last session of the year for a Christmas lunch, or perhaps just a drink?" There were murmurs of assent and for a few minutes the idea was discussed. Eventually, it was decided that all of them, including Ed of course, would go to the Anglesey for an informal lunch on December 22, and Mary and Catherine would book a couple of tables.

It was a pleasant end to the meeting and Lucas drove away in a cheerful mood. Today, he decided, he would have a sandwich lunch in the Stoke Road cafe and treat himself to dinner at The Alverbank in the evening. As he had promised to show Liz some of what he had written for his science-fiction assignment, he had better spend the rest of the day getting on with it, as so far he had only put down an outline. As far as the story went, his first idea had been to write about his own experience of time-travel - in such a way, of course, to imply that it only came from his imagination - but on reflection, he thought it might not be wise to give any hints about his unique position. Instead he had chosen to use the ideas put forward in H. G. Wells' "Time Machine." His hero would travel forward in time from 1881 to the present day, thus making a link with his own adventure but, as it were, in reverse.

Back in his flat, he worked hard on this story throughout the afternoon. Once he had started, ideas began to flow. His nineteenth century character, Robin, began to have some interesting and sometimes amusing adventures after he arrived in 1981. At about half past six, he put down his pen and read through what he had written so far. He felt modestly pleased with the outcome and hoped Liz would feel that it was a decent piece of work when she read it tomorrow. Then he put on his coat and drove to The Alverbank where as ever he enjoyed a delicious meal. I mustn't do this every evening, he chided himself - I must make a real effort to cook myself dinner!

Chapter Thirty-six

As he drove into Gosport next morning to meet Liz, Lucas noticed that Christmas decorations had been put up in the town. These were quite simple affairs, consisting of strings of lights across the High Street together with a large,brightly-lit Christmas tree near the Town Hall. For a moment or two, these reminders of the festive season made Lucas feel rather melancholy. He knew he wouldn't be seeing either his parents or any of his friends this Christmas. Of course, all of the people close to him in 2081 knew that he would be away on this special assignment - but it was particularly hard not to be able to communicate with them at this special time of year.

As he walked towards the little cafe, Lucas put aside these thoughts and began to look forward to seeing Liz and discussing their stories. He went in and ordered coffee - last time it had been the best he had tasted in 1981 - and it wasn't long before Liz came bustling in to join him. She took some papers out of her bag and sat down.

"Do you smoke, Lucas?" she asked, taking a packet of cigarettes from her handbag. "Oh, yes, occasionally," replied Lucas. "Have one to keep me company. I find smoking helps me to concentrate on my writing - at least, that's my excuse!" she smiled. Once again, Lucas was struck by how common this habit, long prohibited by 2081, was at this period in time.

They exchanged their science-fiction stories and quietly read through each other's work. "You can keep mine," said Liz, "it's a copy - I was able to use our new photocopying machine in the library!"

Lucas was very impressed with Liz's story. She had written about a very elderly woman who was sitting in her garden thinking about some happier times in her life. Into the garden came a much younger woman who she did not know, and who gave the old lady a strange glowing glass sphere before hurrying away. When the woman looked into the sphere she saw moving images of herself as a younger person......

Lucas put down the story. "This is really good, Liz!" he exclaimed. "What a brilliant start!"

Liz blushed with pleasure. "It's just a starting idea," she said, "I'm still trying to work out how to continue it. Do you honestly think that it's O.K.?"

"Absolutely!" said Lucas, "You really do have a talent for writing. And I shall want to read it all when you've finished it!"

"Well, thank you kind sir!" she said, "I'm going to say the same thing about your story. I think you've actually made the idea of someone arriving in the present day from another time totally believable. It's very good and..." She paused for a moment and continued, "Your hero is very convincing....it's almost as though it's something you might have experienced yourself."

She put down the story and gazed across at him. They were silent for a moment. Lucas almost wanted to tell this perceptive girl the truth. But he dare not, even though he knew she had picked up some fragment of the mystery Liz broke the silence.

"Must go back to work now," she said. "I hope you will tell me some more about yourself the next time we meet." And then she smiled. "Forgive me if I've been too personal, Lucas. Just my writer's imagination I suppose. Thank you, it's been great sharing our stories."

She reached across the table and squeezed his hand. "I reckon we're both on the way to becoming great literary stars!"

"Let's meet again Liz!" he said and she smiled in agreement before picking up her things and leaving the cafe. After she had gone, Lucas sat there lost in thought stirring his cold coffee.

Chapter Thirty-seven

Eventually Lucas drove slowly back to his flat. Having parked the Fiesta he walked back out to the shops, having decided to buy a few snacks and a bottle of decent wine for Beth's visit on the following evening. He went to the "Bluebird" cafe on the front to have a late lunch and was soon enjoying a warming meal of cheese on toast and a pot of tea. Catching sight of himself in the mirror behind the counter, he realised that it was really about time he had his hair cut - he felt that he looked unkempt and scruffy and after all, he wanted to look his best when Beth came to visit him. So after finishing his meal, he walked along to Curzon's large "Unisex" hairdressing salon, the one he had noticed on his first visit to Lee. Inside, the pleasant middle-aged receptionist welcomed him and although there were no appointments available that afternoon, booked him in for a trim and tidy-up at 11.15 on the following day.

It would be an interesting experience, Lucas thought, wondering how it would compare to hairdressing techniques that he knew from his own time. Back in the flat he added a few notes to his thesis and started to write more in his personal journal. Presently he put down his pen and spent a contemplative hour thinking about his present situation.

It was not easy to work out his thoughts and feelings just now. Whenever he was on his own for long periods, like now, he missed the conveniences and pleasures of 2081. The comfortable things he had taken for granted - a super-clean house with all the conveniences of the late twenty-first century, his computers, his multi-purpose phone with instant access to social media and information, the facilities to travel quickly and easily - in fact, his whole life had been tailored to his individual requirements. None of these things were now available to him. But as soon as he was in the company of the new acquaintances he had come to know, he forgot about these things that he used to take for granted and he became filled with a different kind of vitality. As he gazed around his simple 1981 flat, he knew he must learn to reconcile his difficulties and try to feel more positive. After all, no-one else that he knew had had the chance to live a life in the past. It was up to him to make the absolute most of it.

And what about his growing relationships with both Beth and Liz? They were very different women. He felt he understood Liz a little better, but then they had got to know each other through their shared interest in writing. Yes, he did find her attractive, but at least so far they were getting to know each other just through talking and expressing their ideas and feelings. It was very different with Beth. What had happened there was a powerful and passionate need for each other. He loved being in the company of both women. Did he have the right, though, to interfere with their lives, as this was their time, not his? Before he had come to 1981, he had believed - supported by his training and objective background - that he would assume a cool, detached attitude towards the people he would meet. But in truth, this had not happened. And he could not change the events that he had put into being

- and he did not want to. It was best to let fate take its course.

Eventually Lucas put aside his metaphysical musings and turned to the mundane but necessary task of making himself something to eat. He cooked a meal such as many other single flat-dwellers might - bacon and eggs, with some oven chips. Rudimentary as it was, he was pleased with his culinary effort. Afterwards, like many others on this cold December night in 1981, he settled down in his comfortable old armchair to watch television. He was quite impressed with a programme entitled M.A.S.H., a dark comedy concerning a team of American doctors at a mobile hospital in South Korea during the Korean war of the 1950s. Next he watched another historical drama, *The Borgias*, set in fifteenth century Italy. Both of these serials were quite impressive in their own way, he thought. After this rather serious stuff, he ended his evening's viewing with a relaxing hour of snooker. This early television coverage of the this sport, he reflected, had made the game internationally popular and snooker continued to draw in large crowds in his own time.

Chapter Thirty-eight

Lucas rose quite early next morning. As he performed his normal washing rituals, as always he missed being able to have a shower. He wondered whether he should buy one of those contraptions he had seen advertised, a rather primitive-looking shower system whereby two hoses could be fitted to the bath taps. It would be a change, he thought, from having to have a bath all the time. After he had dressed and eaten breakfast, he switched on the radio - not many stations on there in these days - and listened to Radio One for a while before going out for his appointment at the hairdresser's.

The receptionist introduced him to a very pretty young woman who showed him to a chair near the long window.

"Good morning!" she said brightly. "I'm Aureole. Now what can I do for you? Just a trim, or a new style perhaps?"

"Oh, just a trim I think. I'm Lucas, by the way. Aureole! That's an unusual name," he smiled.

"I know!" she laughed. "And your name is too!" This light-hearted exchange immediately led to a relaxed mood as Aureole made a start on his hair. It was a very different experience to what Lucas was accustomed to in his own time - in 2081, he could look at holographic images of himself with various hair styles, and the whole process of hairdressing took place in individual rooms with ambient music in the background. Here in 1981, there was only a mirror to show him how his hair looked. Nevertheless, Aureole was an expert hairdresser. She worked quickly and neatly and when she had finished Lucas was very impressed with the result and complimented her warmly.

"Thank you!" she smiled, "but it was easy to keep the shape of your hair, I only had to trim it. Can I ask you, wherever did you have your hair done last time? Whoever did it made an excellent job of it!"

"Oh," said Lucas, "I had it done at Zahar's...er, in London."

"Zahar's...." she mused, "I haven't heard of that particular salon. Well, they've certainly done a great job with your hair - what a stylish cut!"

"And you've done a great job too!" said Lucas truthfully. "And while I'm staying here, I shall definitely come to you again!"

Aureole led him back to the reception desk, and before she went off he pressed two 50p coins into her hand for a tip.

"Why, that's most generous of you Lucas!" she exclaimed, "Thank you!" He turned to the receptionist - and now it was his turn to be surprised.

"That will be £1.25, please, sir," she said, "I'm sorry, our prices have just gone up recently."

"Well, that's really good value," said Lucas, who, still a little unaccustomed to prices in 1981, was amazed at how cheap it seemed -haircuts in his own time cost between £60 and £100! No wonder that Aureole was pleased with her £1 tip!

It was now lunchtime and Lucas thought that he would try somewhere different. He drove into Gosport to see what the T & J Chinese restaurant in the little shopping precinct had to offer. After parking the Fiesta in the large car park behind the High Street - which, he noticed, bore the legend "Shop in Gosport and Lee where car parking's free!" - he walked along to the precinct. He studied the menu in the window of the restaurant which offered a three-course lunch for a mere £2.99. Soon he was enjoying a delicious meal of tomato soup, followed by lemon chicken with chips with raspberry cheesecake for sweet. It was a most pleasant experience and he left the restaurant feeling warm and well-fed.

Back at the flat, he busied himself making the place warm and welcoming for Beth's visit in the evening. In the late afternoon he made himself a couple of sandwiches. Then he bathed, shaved again and changed into his best casual clothes. He tried to settle down ready for Beth's appearance. Time seemed to pass so slowly. He checked his watch over and over again. 8.15....8.30....9 o'clock. He looked out of the window several times. It was now half-past nine - surely she would be here in a minute? Then, just as he had started to think that she wasn't coming at all, he heard a light knock at the door and there she was. He embraced her as she stepped inside in a warm haze of perfume and sherry.

"I'm sorry I'm a bit late," she said, "I thought it would look a bit odd if I didn't go to the pub with the others for a little while!"

"Doesn't matter Beth, you're here now and it's good to see you - you look absolutely fabulous!" he cried. She permitted a quick kiss and hug before saying, "Let me look at your flat! It's good, and nice and warm here..... you have done yourself proud!"

Beth took off the white faux-fur coat he liked so much and sat on the sofa. Lucas brought over a glass of wine for each of them and it was not long before they began to kiss passionately. Swiftly they moved into the bedroom for a thrilling session of love-making.

Afterwards they lay together warm and contented. "That was wonderful Lucas!" breathed Beth, "so much more comfortable than in the car!"

He held her tightly. "Beth, I don't want you to go," he said.

"You know I must! But I'd like a quick coffee before I go," she said. So Lucas went off to make the drinks and soon they were sitting at the table, sipping their coffees. They spoke briefly about the upcoming party on Saturday. "Remember, Lucas," said Beth rather seriously, "we must be very careful to behave ourselves - my husband will be there, you know."

Lucas took her down the stairs to see her safely into her car, which she had parked on the main road in front of the Post Office.

"Lucas, it's so cold out here, don't hang about, go on in! I'll be fine!" she cried. But of course he did not, but stayed out in the road waving as she drove away quickly.

Back inside Lucas sat on the sofa in a warm and happy daze. At last he stirred himself and began to tidy up, noting with sentimental pleasure the ring of lipstick round the top of Beth's wine glass. What a wonderful way to start life in his new flat! He fell asleep quickly, his dreams full of Beth.

Chapter Thirty-nine

On Friday morning, Lucas wrote down his thoughts about the precious evening in his personal journal. He tried to analyse his feelings about Beth. He felt overwhelmed with love for her, he wanted to be with her all the time. But he knew this was impossible - she was a married woman and what was more, he did not truly belong to this world. He knew he must somehow try to make sure he was not a burden to Beth. But of course he desired to continue their wonderful sexual affair. For the moment, he decided, he should just let fate decide the outcome.

After he had written about last night, he found himself wishing once again that mobile phones had been around in 1981 so that he could be in touch with her. It seemed hard, and even uncivil rather, not to be able to text Beth to express his happiness about last night. But it was idle to worry about it and he turned to the practical task of making himself some sandwiches for lunch.

In the afternoon he decided to go for a long walk in the cold, crisp air. For some time now, he had felt the need to do more exercise. In 2081, like almost everybody else, he had belonged to a gym which he had used regularly. He had had a personalised programme there, adapted to his needs and had been accustomed to walk, run and cycle to aid his desire to keep fit. But here, in the late twentieth century, it seemed that such things were not common.

He had heard talk of aerobics, dance exercise and other such things but very little about organised methods of keeping fit. However, a good long walk would have to do for now, he thought, even though he didn't possess any really appropriate sportswear. Presently he was walking at a steady pace along the main road towards Stubbington before returning across the park down to the seafront at Hillhead and then back to Lee. Dusk was falling as he returned to the flat, invigorated and glowing from his long walk.

He cooked some potatoes and added them to a healthy-looking salad which he enjoyed before settling down in the armchair with a glass of wine, wishing that Beth was here again. Still, he would be seeing her at the party tomorrow night. How would it turn out, he wondered? For tonight, he would try to relax in front of the television.

The first show he watched was a pleasant 'sit-com' about a suburban couple called Terry and June, which he knew to be very popular at this time. He found it quite amusing and rather pleasant, its easy-going gentleness in sharp contrast to the harsher style of shows of this type in his own time. Next he changed the channel to BBC-2 where he watched a programme about a new nature conservation area known as Woods Mill in Sussex and the people who ran it. Such early schemes as these, he thought, had been vital in the development of the ideas of conservation in the late twentieth century. These early pioneers would be pleased to know that this place would still be flourishing a century later. He completed his evening's viewing by watching the coverage of the United Kingdom Snooker Final. The two finalists, attired in dark, formal suits and crisp shirts complete with bow ties, showed their skills to a quiet but enthralled audience, most of whom were also smartly dressed for the occasion. A hundred years later snooker was still a very popular sport, although its presentation had become more flashy and the game itself tended to be played more quickly. Lucas found this earlier version of the game most agreeable and relaxing.

After the snooker coverage finished, he turned off the set and read through the Gosport and Fareham local handbooks he had bought from the shop downstairs the other day. In the Fareham one he saw an advertisement and a small feature about the Leisure Centre. This place, he read, had only been open for about a year. He decided he would pay a visit to the centre tomorrow - he would be able to have a swim and look around to see the other fitness facilities that were on offer.

Chapter Forty

Lucas set off early on Saturday morning to visit the Leisure Centre. It would be most interesting to see this place, a prototype of the large gymnasia that existed everywhere in 2081. After parking his car, he went to the reception desk to book for a swim and before going to the changing rooms he walked around the centre to see what else was on offer. There was a series of rooms named The Bodymatters Health and Fitness Suite, where he could see a few people exercising on various pieces of equipment, including a treadmill and a rowing machine. There was an indoor bowls pitch and also squash and badminton courts. On a central notice board, among other announcements he noticed an advertisement for The Over 50s Health and Fun Club. There was also a large bar and a cafe. Lucas thought the whole place looked welcoming; the decor was bright and the open-plan design allowed for good viewing of the activities.

He was a good swimmer and having changed, made his way to the main pool - there was a smaller one for learners he noticed - and swam some strong lengths. Feeling invigorated, he left the water, changed back again and spent some time in the bar which overlooked the pool. He had enjoyed his experience and knew he would come back again. Maybe, he thought, he could play a game of squash or badminton. He would ask if any of the people in the operatic group might care for a game at some time.

He stayed on in Fareham for lunch. He parked in the new multi-storey car park - only 10p for the day! - and walked downstairs into the shopping precinct where he had a meal in the Garden Cafe. He enjoyed watching the bustle of the many shoppers all around. Yet again, he found it odd that no-one at all was using a mobile phone.

After a short look around the precinct, Lucas drove home to prepare for the enticing prospect of this evening's party. After some thought, he decided that he would walk to the party - he was always worried about the risks of drinking and driving, although it was obvious that this did not seem to bother most of the people he had come to know in 1981. So, wrapped up well against the December cold, he set off to walk along the main road from Lee. It was quite easy to locate Vernon's house on Privett Road as there were already several cars parked along the main road. Vernon's wife, Patricia, welcomed him into the warm house where there were already about twenty people mingling in small groups. Soon Lucas was chatting to a couple of his friends from the operatic society. Gradually the rooms filled up as more people arrived, including some neighbours and some folks from Vernon's workplace. It was interesting, Lucas noted, that there wasn't a great deal of interaction between the different groups. The opera people tended to stick together, having so much in common with each other.

Chapter Forty-one

About half an hour after he had been there, Lucas saw Beth and her husband arrive. Of course, she looked stunning. She was wearing a smart low-cut black dress, high heels and silver-coloured jewellery including some striking hooped ear-rings. Martin, her husband, was tall, neatly attired and looked quite young. After a while, Beth and Martin came over to join Lucas' group which consisted of Barry, June, Bob, Sharon, Belinda and Ray. While Beth chattered brightly, Martin seemed, as Lucas had expected, to be rather distant and uncommunicative. Lucas knew that he must not appear to be too interested in Beth, even though she was the absolute centre of his thoughts. So after a few minutes, he moved along to a group of other people that he did not know. Soon he was enjoying a conversation with Vernon's next-door neighbours whose names were Judith and Trevor. They were an engaging couple. It turned out that Judith owned a dress shop in Stoke Road.

"You know, Lucas, it's rather interesting," she said at one point, "your surname - Mallon - there was a girl called Elaine working in my shop up to a couple of years ago and she got married to a young chap called Brian Mallon. Is he any relation of yours, perhaps? I think he's a teacher. They've got a little baby now and I believe they still live locally."

For a moment Lucas could not speak. Then, aware that

Judith was looking at him quizzically, obviously expecting a response, he managed to mumble rather lamely, "Er, I don't know him, he might be a distant cousin perhaps." His mind was in a whirl. At one time, he had briefly tried to research his family tree. He was pretty sure that his great-grandfather had been named Brian. It was quite possible that this ancestor was alive at this time in the past - he had never thought of such an occurrence before.

But this was no time to start pondering on this strange revelation. Fortunately, Judith did not seem to notice his discomfiture and was carrying on chatting about her shop and business in the town in general. After a little more conversation, Lucas excused himself and went into the kitchen to collect another drink and a plate of the plentiful food that was on offer. He was soon joined by his hostess, Patricia.

"Lucas!" she cried, "Why are you lurking in here on your own? Come and have a dance with me!" She steered him into the dimly-lit smaller room off the lounge where five or six couples were dancing to some slow music emanating from the record player. No-one in the room seemed to be dancing with their partners or wives, he observed. There was a sensuous mood and Patricia was very flirtatious, holding him close.

"You're very quiet, Lucas," she whispered in his ear. "You're so mysterious. Lots of us women are very interested in you." Her teasing words made him feel confident.

"Well, you're all very interesting too," he said.

"All?" she whispered back. "No, not all of us - just one in particular. We've all noticed!" He began to deny it, but she interrupted him. "Never mind about her at the moment. Shut up and kiss me!"

Lucas did as he was told. He was feeling quite excited by this sudden intimacy. Suddenly he felt a light kick on the back of his leg. Breaking away briefly from Patricia, he realised that it had been Beth who had tapped him with one of her high heeled shoes. Through the dimness he saw she was dancing nearby with Pete, one of the younger chorus members. She wasn't cross with him, was she? After all, she had told him to be careful this evening, particularly with regard to her.......

When the music ended, he stepped back from Patricia and asked her if he could get her a drink. "Yes, anything," she said, "as long as it's alcoholic!" He went to the kitchen and poured out a couple of glasses of white wine for them both. Rather to his amusement, when he returned to the darkened room with the drinks, Patricia was now entwined around Bob while Beth was sitting down just outside the room and talking to Martin. Neither of the women paid any attention to Lucas. I've never really understood women and I probably never will, he thought ruefully.

Lucas went into the lounge and sat down for a while, chatting to Barry and his wife Joanna. Presently the were joined by Jane, a small, attractive woman with bouffant hair. She was one of the ladies of the chorus who he had not previously met. They began to discuss their plans for Christmas and Lucas admitted, truthfully, that he did not yet know what he would be doing over the festive season. After a while, he went into the kitchen to refill his glass and as he was doing so, Beth appeared at his side.

"Lucas!" she said brightly. "Have you got a cigarette? I really fancy one!" As he lit one for her, she said, "Martin disapproves of me smoking - so I'd better go outside and have it - come and join me for a minute!"

Of course he was delighted with this subterfuge. They stepped out of the back door. It was freezing outside, but he didn't care for at once they were kissing passionately.

"Oh God, Lucas, I want you," she gasped huskily.

"Beth, come to me in the flat next week, I want you too!" he whispered.

"I'll come as soon as I can - I'll work on it," she said, "and now I must go back. And thank you for being careful tonight and not being possessive." At the door, she turned and flashed him a smile. "And leave that Patricia alone!"

This brief encounter had made Lucas feel very happy. He helped himself to another drink and chatted to Vernon, who asked him what he thought about the opera group in general. He went back into the lounge and sat down with Belinda, Ray, Bob, Sarah and Jane. In a little while, Beth came over to the group with her coat over her arm.

"Beth!" cried Belinda, "Surely you're not leaving just yet? It's only just gone eleven!" Beth made a face.

"Yes, we're off. Martin's bored. You know he doesn't exactly understand parties and he's ready to go home, so I'd better keep him sweet." And off she went to join Martin who was standing by the door. "Night night!" she called, and looked back towards Lucas with a wide smile.

After Beth and Martin had left, there was some talk among the little group about how, on the whole, husbands or wives of various members of the operatic society did not really understand the attitudes and feelings of their other halves. Lucas became irritated because Belinda and Ray voiced some criticisms of Beth. I know her far better than any of you, he thought. Impulsively, he asked Jane if she would like to dance - she, at least, had not joined in the gossip. Soon they were entwined quite closely together to slow and moody music. He found this experience exciting, whilst at the same time his mind was fascinated by the apparent ease with which these sexual flirtations were so prevalent. Surely he shouldn't have kissed Jane? Perhaps he was drunk. Jane certainly was.

But after a couple of close embraces, Jane suddenly pulled away and they went into the kitchen for another drink. They smoked and talked for a while. Lucas found out that Jane was a secretary at a car hire firm and he in turn told her about his thesis work.

"You know, Lucas," she said, slurring her words, "you really are a bit of a mystery man."

Where have I heard that before? thought Lucas. But he replied, "No, nothing mysterious about me - nothing at all. Except that....." and he paused for dramatic effect -

"except that....I travelled back in time, just so that I could see what all you lot were up to!"

At this, Jane burst into laughter and so too did Belinda, who had appeared by his side at that moment. "Well," cried Belinda, "that explains why you're so weird!" And the three of them laughed again. In Vino Veritas, thought Lucas. But in a way he was relieved to have spoken the truth for once, even though neither Belinda nor Jane would believe it of course.

The party began to wind down towards one in the morning. He said his goodnights to everyone and walked home. So many thoughts swirled round in his head; Judith's revelations about his possible great-grandfather, the dynamics of the party, Beth and her husband, his dalliance with Jane, the sexiness of the whole evening. His flat seemed dull and quiet when he arrived there. He made himself a hot chocolate drink and flopped into the armchair before retiring. It was some time before he fell asleep, many images from the party going round in his mind. Eventually, he slept deeply, waking quite late on Sunday morning, and, happily, feeling better than he thought he might!

Chapter Forty-two

Lucas spent a quiet day on Sunday, interspersing writing in his journals with a ride out to the Old Lodge to treat himself to a good lunch. In the warmth and pleasant ambience of the hotel, he found himself wondering about what all the people he had met at the party were doing today. He realised that he had been living in 1981 for a month now. So much had happened since he arrived! It was still so strange to be part of two timelines. Just now his existence in 2081 seemed like a dream that was beginning to fade away - there was so much to fill his life here at the moment, despite the inconveniences and difficulties he faced at times. And then there had been Judith's revelation about the baby boy that might well be his great-grandfather.......

Back at the flat, he decided it was time to make a few improvements to make the place more personal and comfortable and next morning he set out to buy a few things to make the place more of a home. He drove to Fareham, parked in the multi-storey car park and browsed around the precinct and West Street.

First he bought a rather decent bookshelf from a large second-hand shop and having taken it back to put in the boot of the Fiesta, returned to buy some books . He was impressed to discover that Fareham had three bookshops - in his own time such places were rare indeed, since nearly everybody bought their reading matter on line - and spent an enjoyable time choosing books from all of them. He bought a book called *Future Shock* by Alvin Toffler which contained some interesting views concerning possible coming trends for the twenty-first century. His other purchases included a history of the Gilbert and Sullivan operas, a book about "body language", and a sociological tome called "The Theory Of Communicative Action" which he thought would be useful for his studies. In addition he bought a varied selection of paperback novels, including some from a charity shop. Next he found a shop that sold art prints and chose a couple of framed pictures - a Monet and an Edward Hopper - to brighten up his flat.

Having taken these new purchases back to the car, he returned to the precinct and the Garden Cafe where he enjoyed a sandwich while he read his newspaper. It had been a long, tiring but productive morning. He finished his shopping by choosing a couple of small table lamps, a bright hearth rug and some little silver ornaments before driving home. He carried his new purchases up to the flat - he would sort them all out tomorrow. Soon it would be time for the operatic rehearsal.

Chapter Forty-three

Beth had told Lucas that she couldn't meet him before the rehearsal this evening, as she had to work late and would have to hurry to get down to the hall tonight. But at the party she had said that she would try to work out some way of seeing him this week, so he knew they would have to find a moment together on their own. At the start of the rehearsal Andy announced that they would practice some of the chorus numbers in the first half before trying a run out of Act One on the stage after the break. Lucas enjoyed the music as usual as Andy conducted the singing with discipline. It so happened that Beth was one of the people on tea-duty tonight, and when he reached the counter during the break, she whispered, "Meet you in your car after the pub."

Andrea took over the rehearsal for the second half, working out the moves for the chorus and principals all the way through till ten o'clock. "Thank you all for your hard work tonight!" she said, "and remember - it's a men-only rehearsal on Thursday - the ladies can have an evening off!"

The hall emptied and Lucas strolled along cheerfully with the others to the welcome warmth of the pub. The seating arrangements were more or less the same as usual and they soon settled down with their drinks. Beth was sitting next to Belinda, with Calvin and young Pete on each side of the two women, while Lucas sat opposite alongside Vernon, Bob, Patricia and Barry. They were soon discussing Saturday's party, which was generally assumed to have been a success.

"Enjoy it, Lucas?" asked Vernon. "Oh yes, it was really good!" replied Lucas.

"Ha! I saw you getting off with Jane!" cried Belinda, to his annoyance - this encounter with Jane had occurred after Beth had left on Saturday and he was immediately worried about how she might react. But Beth didn't seem fazed by it.

"Well, we all had our moments!" said Bob cheerfully.

"You certainly did, Belinda! I saw you trying to seduce my husband!" cried Patricia.

"Oh," laughed Belinda, "I was a bit worse for wear - it could have been anybody!"

"Well, thank you very much!" chortled Vernon, "and there I was, thinking my tremendous sex appeal was working really well!"

"H'mm," said Beth, "my moments were few and far between. I'm not bringing Martin with me again!"

They all laughed and as the gossip about the party continued, Lucas thought that the various sexual dalliances that had occurred on Saturday hadn't really amounted to anything serious - unless the jolly bonhomie was covering up some deeper feelings?

When the landlord called, "Time, ladies and gentlemen please!" the groups rose reluctantly to leave."

"See you Thursday, Lucas!" said Barry, "but a bloody men only rehearsal - not so good without the ladies!"

"Oh, you'll manage," said Patricia, "it's time you men did some hard work to keep you up to our standard!". They all went their separate ways and Lucas got into the Fiesta and waited for Beth to join him. Soon she was climbing into the passenger seat and quickly they were hugging and kissing.

Beth broke away and said breathlessly, "I've had a great idea Lucas - can you meet me in the daytime on Wednesday? I am owed a day off at work and I can take it then. I've already told Martin that I'm seeing Belinda for lunch that day - she'll vouch for me!"

Lucas was thrilled. "Beth, that's marvellous - of course we can meet - I'll pick you up - what time? " "How about 11.30? We could have a pub lunch - and then go back to your flat - if you like?"

Lucas was filled with happiness and excitement. "Where would you like to go for lunch?" he asked. "I don't mind. You choose. So long as you get me back home by about four so I have time to recover!" she said brightly. And after another long kiss, Beth hurried off to her own car. What a wonderful girl, thought Lucas as he drove home, amazed and delighted that she had gone to so much trouble to give them the opportunity for what promised to be a wonderful day together.

Chapter Forty-four

Next morning Lucas drove out to the Thorngate Halls for his regular writers' group meeting. Today, Ed the tutor had an unusual assignment for each of the members. He handed each of them a different picture postcard.

"You will see that all of these postcards have been posted to various people from different holiday destinations. Note that each card has a message of some sort to the recipient," he said. "Now, what I would like each of you to do is to spend the hour before the break in writing either about the person or persons who sent the card and what they have been doing on holiday. Or, if you prefer, you could write about what the recipient thought when they received the card. Of course, you will use the message on the card as a guide. Basically, the idea is to expand what is written into a wider form - to create a longer story than that which appears on the card."

"Can we invent something that they might have done but not written about?" asked Mary. "Certainly," replied Ed, "so long as there is some connection with what is written on the postcard."

The group set to work. Lucas' card had been sent by 'Mum and Dad' to their married daughter in Portsmouth. The card depicted a fine, sunny day on the beach at Bournemouth, the sands full of holidaymakers. The message read, "Enjoying the change, though the weather not great. Lively hotel, food is o.k. Am just off to look round the shops, dad's having a rest this p.m. Hope you're keeping well, see you when we get back on Saturday. Love, Mum & Dad." Lucas decided to write about what 'Dad' might actually be thinking about this holiday. He began by writing: "Yes, I am having a rest in our room - got hardly any sleep last night with that horrible lot on their stag night shouting along the corridors. And it's rained ever since we've got here......" Lucas carried along in this vein, writing an imaginary account of Dad's grumbles. He found it fun to do!

During the break he sat next to Liz and they talked about their efforts this morning with the postcards. Liz had had a postcard from a woman who was enjoying a holiday in Austria. The writer had written in quite a lot of detail about her sight seeing. Liz had chosen to record the recipient's thoughts on reading her friend's descriptions - she had imagined that the woman who had received the card felt a little jealous as she had been unable to take a holiday herself.

By the time they had talked about their writing, the coffee break was nearly over. Lucas suggested they could have a lunchtime drink after class and Liz readily accepted the offer. Back in the Rogers Room, Ed asked each of the members of the group to read out the written messages on the cards and then what they had written about them themselves. It was an enjoyable session - Ed pronounced himself very pleased with the efforts. Towards the end of the meeting, he led a general discussion on how similar much of the content was in the tradition of postcard writing.

After the class broke up, Lucas drove Liz to the White Hart. She told him that she would only stay for a short time, as she had to be at the library for her afternoon shift.

"Don't you have any time then for a lunch on Tuesdays?" asked Lucas.

"No," she replied, "I take sandwiches in and eat them at work while I get the chance!"

The pub was quiet and Lucas bought them both a glass of wine and packet of crisps and soon they were talking about the progress of their science fiction stories. In some way, Lucas had the feeling that their light-hearted chat was acting as a cover for deeper thoughts and feelings. It was really strange to sit with this young woman who would one day become a celebrated author. He could tell that Liz was sensing that he had a secret - and that in some strange way, she could tell that he knew something about her too.

And, sure enough, she looked across at him and said quietly, "I wish you would tell me what it is you're hiding from me, Lucas."

"What makes you say that?" he said lightly.

"Well.....among other things...this is just an example..... we've both lived in this place all our lives, but to me, I find living here quite dull, really.. I mean, it's o.k., but all a bit mundane and samey. Yet it's clear that you find everything so fascinating! I noticed how, when we came in here, you take in everything, you examine things, like the beer mats, the crisp bags, the whole surroundings..... it's as though you've never seen them before!"

He held her gaze steadily, not quite knowing how to reply. But just as he was trying to work out what his response should be, Liz glanced at her watch. "Goodness - look at the time! We must go!" she cried.

They hurried out of the pub and got into the Fiesta. He drove them along Stoke Road and into the High Street. Both Liz and Lucas were quiet on the short journey, lost in their own thoughts. When they arrived, Lucas opened the passenger door.

As she stepped out, he said impulsively, "Liz, would you care to come out and have a meal with me somewhere on Saturday night?"

She gave him a warm smile. "Lucas, thank you - I'd love to! And you can decide where we shall go!" Quickly, they agreed that he would pick her up from her flat at half past seven. She walked in to the library, turning to wave at him.

As he drove back towards Lee, Lucas worried briefly that perhaps he had made a mistake in asking Liz out. But then, he mused, this was a natural development of a relationship; both of them obviously found each other interesting to talk to. It was, he concluded, a very different kind of friendship compared with the more sexual one he enjoyed with Beth. He turned his attention to practical matters. He stopped off in Stoke Road where he had earlier noticed a sportswear shop. Inside, he bought himself a blue tracksuit and a pair of decent running shoes to equip himself better for his running exercises. Back in the flat, he put up his new bookshelves and arranged the books neatly, adding the two new silver ornaments to the shelves. Then he hung the two framed pictures on the long wall before placing one of the new lamps on top of the bookcase and the other on the small table next to the sofa. Once he had placed the new rug in front of the sofa, he switched on the small lights just as dusk was falling. He was pleased with his efforts - the flat looked much more homely and comfortable. He cooked himself an evening meal of bacon, eggs and tomatoes and spent a pleasant evening writing up his course notes and personal journal while playing his E.L.O. and Mott the Hoople records. It had been a good day and he was looking forward so much to seeing Beth tomorrow.

Chapter Forty-five

Next morning, before leaving to pick up Beth, Lucas made sure the flat was looking tidy and fiddled with the heater to make sure it would be warm enough to welcome them both back in the afternoon. He had decided to take Beth for lunch at the Bun Penny. He drove carefully to Beth's home, which was a little modern house along a small road just south of Fareham. As soon as he arrived, Beth appeared at the door and hurried out to the car. She looked great, thought Lucas, and he told her so. "Thanks Lucas," she smiled, "I've been looking forward to this all morning! Where are you taking me?" "I thought we might go to the Bun Penny again," said Lucas. "That's great! I like it there!" she said brightly. Soon they were bowling along towards the pub to the accompaniment of one of Lucas' tapes.

"Ah! The Move"! I once went to see them in Portsmouth a few years ago!" cried Beth "Which other groups do you like, Lucas?"

"Oh, quite a few," answered Lucas, "I like E.L.O., Mott the Hoople, Queen, The Pet Shop Boys..."

"Pet Shop Boys?" frowned Beth, "what an odd name for a group - I must say, I've never heard of them!"

"Oh, they're quite new," said Lucas hurriedly, realising rather too late that the duo had not been around in 1981..

157

They chatted on about music for a little while, Lucas making sure not to commit any other *faux-pas*.

Soon they had arrived at the Bun Penny. They hurried inside to the welcoming warmth of the old pub and soon were sitting at a side table in the main bar enjoying their first schooners of sherry. Beth was wearing a dark red dress, stylishly cut, and Lucas noticed her fine eye make-up and her red painted finger nails. She told him how good it was to be taken out. She was obviously feeling relaxed and happy and Lucas knew they were going to have a great time. They decided to have sandwiches rather than a full meal. While they ate, Beth told Lucas much more about her life - about her enjoyment of singing, about her habit of day-dreaming and - this surprised Lucas - how she lacked confidence in herself.

"But I love being in the shows," she said, "to me, there's nothing better than being up on the stage. You'll love being in *H.M.S. Pinafore* when we get round to performing in front of the audience."

She talked a lot as they drank their way through the bottle of white wine. At one point, she looked across at Lucas with quite a serious face.

"To change the subject," she said, "I wonder...can we just talk about our relationship for a moment? I worry a bit - how can I put this without sounding too negative - I worry that you might be getting too serious with how you think of me. Don't get me wrong - this situation we have between us, we are having good times; I suppose what I'm trying to say is, well, I don't want you to fall in love with me or anything..."

"Oh, Beth," said Lucas earnestly, "I can handle it - I promise I won't overdo things. But you are gorgeous! And I want us to carry on so much!"

"And so do I!" she said, "you know, when I see you in a group, talking to other people, I think to myself, I have something special with that man! It's a good feeling."

"Beth, I feel just the same!" he said. "And really, I'm so glad we have been able to talk about our feelings this way."

The conversation turned to discussing their friends in the operatic society. The bright, cheerful mood permeated the rest of afternoon, aided by an extra glass of wine each. Presently Beth looked up at the large clock on the wall nearby. "Are you going to take me back to your flat?" she whispered, "because I mustn't be late getting back home."

Back in the car, they kissed hungrily before Lucas drove back carefully to Lee. Soon they were hurrying up the staircase to the flat, where they fell upon each other and had an exciting and passionate time in bed. After a while, Lucas reluctantly left the bed and made Beth and himself a strong cup of coffee.

As they sat and sipped their drinks at the table Beth sighed, "I wish I could stay - I'd love to spend the night with you here. But I've got to get back and be a dutiful little wife and make Martin's dinner before he gets in."

"Beth, won't he notice that...that you're different to how you usually are?" asked Lucas a little anxiously.

"No, not him!" she replied wryly. "He never really notices anything about me!" She put down her cup. "And now take me home please. It's been such a great day!"

They walked down to the car and Lucas drove them back to Fareham. At the end of Beth's road, they had the briefest of kisses before she left and disappeared into her house. Lucas drove back to his flat in something of a daze. It had been a wonderful day with his lover - and how quickly time had flown! What a pity that tomorrow night's rehearsal was only for the men. As Beth had said earlier, it would look very odd if she came to meet him in the pub afterwards, but at least they could meet early on the following Monday.

In the evening Lucas sat in the flat in a happy, reflective mood. Beth's alluring perfume was everywhere. He played through the exact tape that he had had on in the car when she was sitting next to him. He wanted to hold this perfect day in his mind for ever. He had promised Beth that he would not fall in love with her - but, he thought to himself, his reactions tonight were just those of a man in love.

Chapter Forty-six

Thursday dawned cold and grey. After the excitement of yesterday. Lucas felt a bit flat. As ever, he found it disappointing that he couldn't contact Beth to talk about their fun times. He turned to practical matters, replenishing his store of groceries and collecting his clean clothes from the laundry. In the early evening he set out for the "men only" rehearsal at the Bogue Hall. Despite the absence of the ladies, he quite enjoyed the singing and stage work before he went along to The Vine with several of the other men.

I obviously prefer women's company to men's, he thought, as most of the conversation tonight consisted of football, politics and television. However, here and there he picked up some gossip about some of the women. He noticed that Beth didn't really feature in any of the discussions; she was regarded as one of the quiet ones. How little they knew! He wondered what she was doing just now - was she thinking about him? He thought it was easier for him to focus on her, as, unlike everyone else. He had no roots in 1981.

"You're quiet tonight Lucas!" said Barry at one point and he realised he had not contributed much towards the evening's conversation. On the drive back to Lee, he told himself that he really should stop dreaming about Beth so much and get on with living an everyday life.

It was very cold on Friday. Lucas had entertained the idea of having a long drive out into the countryside but his plans were to be forestalled. The Fiesta took a long time to start up and then the engine kept cutting out. He did not have the faintest idea of how to deal with the strange car engines of the 1980s. He managed to get the car as far as Skyways garage, went into the workshop and asked for it to be fixed.

"You'll have to manage without it for the day," said the mechanic who was looking over the car, "but I reckon I could get it fixed up for you later this afternoon. It's a common enough problem......" and he went on to explain what was wrong in terms that meant nothing to Lucas. Vehicles in 2081 were much more reliable, he thought! Finally it was agreed that Lucas should phone the garage in the late afternoon to see if it was ready to collect. So he walked back to his flat as a flurry of snow swirled round, made himself a bacon and egg lunch and promised himself a good evening meal at The Alverbank later when the car was fixed.

He was relieved when he rang the garage at four o'clock to hear that the Fiesta was fixed. He set out at once into the cold, arrived at the garage and paid for the repairs. His bill was rather high, but at least the job was done and having paid in cash, he drove back to Lee, happy to have the car back to normal again. At half past seven, he drove out to The Alverbank. Tonight, the dining room was busy; there was a large party of people out for a pre-Christmas meal as well as three other couples. To start with, Lucas felt rather lonely as he sat at a side table, but this feeling soon passed as he began to enjoy his meal which was up to the hotel's usual high standards.

As he ate, he quietly observed the large group, which, he learned from their conversation, was made up of school teachers. There were five women and four men of various ages. It provided for an interesting experience of social interaction. He noticed that one of the men, perhaps a head of department, seemed dominant in gesture and discussion. One of the women was very quiet and rather shy. Another woman was obviously very close to the man sitting beside her. On the whole, they were a pleasant group and he found himself wondering what each of them would take out of their social evening.

Later, after he had finished his dinner. Lucas went up to the bar to buy a glass of wine. While he was being served, one of the group of teachers joined him. He introduced himself as David and the two men exchanged pleasantries. Lucas learned that the party consisted of the English department from Brune Park Comprehensive School and in return described his project about social interaction.

"Do you always come out for a meal to celebrate Christmas?" asked Lucas.

"We do," replied David, "but the best celebration at Brune Park is always the end of term Christmas lunch! You wouldn't believe some of the things that go on then when everyone's had a few drinks....!"

Lucas was interested to hear these revelations. Compared with his own time, the 1980s really seemed to be quite a licentious age. How dull 2081 society would seem, with its censorious, over-protective attitudes, to most of the people he had become acquainted with in his time here !

Chapte Forty-seven

Next morning, cold as it was, Lucas felt the need to blow away the cobwebs. Donning his new tracksuit and running shoes, he set out to enjoy some vigorous exercise along the seafront. At first, as the cold bit into him, he felt he was out of condition but after a few minutes' running he began to enjoy the exercise. He noticed that one or two passers-by, huddled up against the wind, regarded him in a way which suggested that they thought he was mad! Obviously, he thought, outdoor running in December in 1981 was quite uncommon.

He ran for an hour, covering the distance to Hill Head and then back to Elmore twice over before returning to his flat to bathe and have a sandwich lunch. In the afternoon, he settled down to read the Alvin Toffler book. After a while his thoughts turned to his evening date with Liz. He was still undecided whether or not to tell her the truth about himself. Maybe it would be better just to see how their conversation developed during the evening.

At seven o'clock he put on his best clothes and drove into Gosport to collect Liz from her flat in Seaward Towers, where she lived with her widowed mother. He parked the car outside the large tower blocks. Before going in, he took pleasure in the wintry night scene adjacent to the harbour. The town's large Christmas tree was sparkling at the entrance to the Ferry Gardens, and across the water the lights of Portsmouth twinkled in the cold air. Lucas felt a twinge of strangeness as he observed the flats. By 2081 they were long gone, having been demolished when the harbour area had been hugely redeveloped fifty years earlier. For a moment or two he stood there, musing upon the nature of time and change.

Finally putting aside these philosophical thoughts he strode up to the entrance of Seaward Towers. Inside he located the lift, which fortunately was working tonight - Liz had told him that it was often out of order - and rode up to the eighth floor. He walked along the corridor, knocked on Liz's door and she opened it to admit him. He was introduced to her mother, who rose from the sofa to greet him.

"Hello!" she smiled, "I'm Annette and of course you're the young writer whose ideas have so impressed my daughter!"

"I am so pleased to meet you, Annette!" said Lucas, "but really, it's Liz who has the talents!" It was a relaxed atmosphere inside the little flat which was comfortable and warm. Lucas noticed that there were two very prominent large bookshelves.

Annette noticed his interest in the books. "We read a lot, Lucas," she said, "I'm sure you do too - what type of books do you prefer?"

"Oh, science fiction mostly, I suppose, H.G.Wells, Jack Finney, Silverberg, Asimov, Robert E. Corcoran and so on," he replied, without realising that the latter was an author of the late twenty-first century.

After a few more pleasantries had been exchanged, Lucas and Liz left the flat and stepped out into the night air. Lucas drove the short distance to the Chinese restaurant, which was situated in the little precinct. Liz, he observed, looked specially elegant tonight, her long blonde hair framing her fine-boned face. Lucas felt relaxed. Here he was, in the company of a bright, intelligent young woman with the prospect of an interesting evening ahead. Once inside the restaurant, they were shown to a quiet table for two. Lucas ordered them both a drink and as they studied the menu. Liz took out her cigarettes.

"I know you're only an occasional smoker, Lucas." she said, offering him the packet, "but would you care for one just now?" He accepted a cigarette, still feeling quite wicked as he did so as smoking had been forbidden for over half a century by 2081. However, here in the restaurant in 1981, he noticed that there were smokers on almost every table.

The waiter brought over their first course, As they ate, Liz asked Lucas about the operatic society. After he had talked about his experiences so far in the group, Liz said, "I can tell just how much you enjoy it. You speak so enthusiastically!"

"Yes," admitted Lucas, "and it's not only because I've met some interesting new friends, I love the music and acting too. Liz, do you belong to any other group besides the writers' circle?"

She shook her head. "No. I'm not all that sociable really. I spend most of my spare time writing - or, at least, thinking about writing! In fact, this is the first time I've been out for an evening for ages!"

Liz went on to talk about her work in the library and then their conversation turned to books and writing in general. When the waiter brought their coffees, Liz lit a cigarette and looked at him with a serious expression.

"Now, Lucas," she said quietly, "I think you knew I was going to get round to this.....I would really like you to tell me what it is you're hiding from me. Forgive me, that sounds so rude - but I'm sure there's something and I believe you have been on the verge of telling me for a while. Tell me to shut up if I'm wrong!"

Chapter Forty-eight

Lucas took a deep breath. He hesitated for a few moments. Dare he tell Liz the truth about himself? But she was expecting an answer.

"Liz. You - you are right - I have been hiding something; but it is so strange, unique even - you will be so shocked if I tell you the truth about myself."

She looked across at him levelly. "Please tell me. I don't think it can be anything really bad, can it? I mean, you haven't committed some crime or another? You're not on the run? No. I don't believe it's anything like that. It's something very different, isn't it?" She reached across the table and grasped his hand.

Lucas spoke softly. "It is something very different. Liz - perhaps we should drop talking about this. I'm here and you're here and we're having a lovely evening out...." Liz interrupted him sharply.

"Lucas. I am perhaps more resilient than you think. And I want to know! You're not a mass murderer, a bigamist, a woman in disguise or anything like that. Whatever you have to tell me, I can cope with it!"

For a moment Lucas did not know how to respond. I want to tell her, he thought, but I fear what her reaction will be if I do. But she was speaking again.

"Lucas, I have always had a vivid imagination. That's why I write I suppose. Ever since I was quite young, I have always thought that all the mundane things we see around us are not the only elements of our life here on earth. I hope - believe, even - that there are some things that are unexplainable, that magic exists, that there is so much more to life than we normally realise....."

He regarded her silently and she continued, "I believe that there is something fantastic, amazing, magical that surrounds you. I feel...." - and here she breathed hard and gripped his hand again - "I feel... that you are not from this world!" She sat back and gave a nervous little laugh. "Tell me now if I am right or wrong. Don't joke about it, please. And don't lie!"

He studied her quietly. This is it, he thought. I have to tell her. And I feel a sense of relief. Hesitantly at first, he began his tale. "Liz. I have travelled here, through time, from a hundred years in the future. My home is in Gosport, but in 2081 Through a time-travel device I have been sent here, to 1981, in order to do a field study for my university. I have been here for the last six weeks or so."

Liz said nothing as he continued his story. While he was talking, the surroundings of the restaurant seemed to fade away. When he had finished talking, the two sat in silence for a while. Finally Liz broke the silence.

"Lucas," she said quietly, "I have said to you before, that I knew there was something so different about you. All sorts of ideas went round in my mind; not quite that you are a time-traveller though!" And she relaxed visibly and smiled at him.

"So!" she said brightly. "You are unique! Really unique! And...and I know that what you have just told me as the absolute truth! Thank you for telling me, but of course I am just bursting with questions!"

He smiled back. "Thank you for understanding, Liz!" he said. "I feel so happy that I've finally told my secret!"

"And I'm happy that you shared it with me! Even though it is so hard to take it all in! Lucas, I want to know so much more - but I don't think I can organise my thoughts any more tonight," she said. "Let's go now - it's quite late - and....I think I just want to sit quietly back at home tonight to ponder all these things you have told me!"

Lucas agreed and they made plans to meet at his flat tomorrow afternoon to talk about everything again. They gathered their coats and stood up ready to leave the restaurant, smiling thanks to the manager as they left. This pleasant man, Mr. Choi, held open the door for them to pass through. After they had left, he mused about these customers. What an interesting young couple, he thought to himself. Although they had been light-hearted at first, their conversation had obviously taken a serious turn later in the evening. Had they experienced any difficulties in their relationship? But he thought they would be all right. Time heals all things!

Part Two

Chapter One

During the next few days, Lucas experienced a sense of deep relief. At last, he had told Liz his secret. From now on, he would no longer be alone in this strange world he had inhabited for over a month. He wondered whether it was this sense of release that caused the following days and weeks to pass more quickly - or was it merely the fact that he was becoming more accustomed to living in this time?

His relationships, not just with Liz and Beth, but also with his other new friends in the operatic society, continued along their paths. He experienced one particularly difficult evening with Beth at the Monday evening rehearsal before Christmas. They had met early at the Vine, as usual, but she had acted unexpectedly cool towards him. She told Lucas that Belinda had mentioned that several people had been gossiping about the closeness of her relationship with him. She told him that night that their affair had to end. Lucas did not really know how to respond. He was crestfallen and upset, while at the same time being conscious that once again he had failed to consider Beth's difficulties and feelings about what had happened between them.

But this did not prove to be the end of their love affair. After Lucas had spent a wakeful and unhappy night, to his delight upon returning at lunchtime from some desultory shopping in Lee, he saw Beth's car parked next to his outside the flat. Impulsive as ever, she had come to apologise for her mood and words of the night before. Although she only stayed for a few minutes, Lucas was overjoyed - they had survived the first real crisis of their affair. She wanted to continue seeing him as before. Of course, he was more than happy to carry on meeting her, and they mutually agreed that they must in future talk more truthfully about their feelings.

Four days after Christmas, Beth "invented" an extra rehearsal night. They met at the crowded Vine and had a frivolous and happy time during a long, boozy and smoky evening. On another table were Mary from the operatic group, who lived close by, and her husband, but tonight Beth and Lucas had thrown caution to the winds, neither of them caring who saw them together. After this special evening, they went back to his flat for what Lucas always remembered as their best ever sex session.

Meanwhile, his burgeoning friendship with Liz fulfilled him in a completely different way. After his revelations to her they met often. Liz quickly adjusted to the fact that she knew a man from the future and they had long conversations. Liz had never doubted that Lucas was telling the truth. She had so many questions, not only about the future of the world but also about his own feelings about living here in 1981. But she did not want to know anything he might have discovered about her own fate - so he could not tell her how famous she would one day become. At one point, Lucas explained to her that he would never tell anyone else about his time travelling - it would remain a wonderful and secret bond that would tie them together for all time.

As Christmas approached, rather to his surprise, Lucas became quite involved with the spirit of the festive season. He was pleased to receive cards from some of the people in his groups and bought and gave out some of his own. He bought some decorations and a little tree to cheer up the flat. It would be rather strange to spend Christmas Day alone; it was true that Liz had suggested he might go round to her flat, but he knew that her mother's sister and husband together with their two teenage sons were staying there over Christmas and he did not want to intrude on their family time. Instead, he thought of a way to assuage any feelings of loneliness he might have on Christmas Day - he decided to volunteer his services at St. Faith's Church as a helper on the day with preparing and serving the dinner that was provided for the lonely, elderly and vulnerable of the parish.

Chapter Two

Besides the opera rehearsals and the dates with Beth and Liz, the other main social event for Lucas was the pre-Christmas lunch at the Anglesey Arms with his writers' group. It proved to be an interesting occasion, particularly as he could observe the dynamics of group behaviour while participating in it on a personal level at the same time. As had been already agreed, the members of the group met in the bar and when everyone had arrived, Mary and Catherine led the way into the dining room. Two tables had been reserved for the party. Lucas and Liz made sure they could sit together, and their table was completed by the older men, Geoff and Peter, together with Sheila and Mary. Ed, the tutor, sat at the other table with Jane, Caroline, Catherine, Tom and the rather shy young man Tim.

During the lunch, Lucas noticed that on each of the tables one person tended to dominate the conversations. Seated next to Lucas, George led the way. He had many opinions about politics, social issues, modern life in general. Although there was no real malice in what he had to say, he spent a lot of time harking back to "the good old days". The other older person, Mary, seemed to feel the same way. Lucas concluded that both of them were perhaps wistfully remembering their younger days. However, perhaps this was somewhat of a generalisation - for Peter, who was almost the same age as Geoff, appeared to much more content with his life. On the other table, it was quite apparent that Ed held full sway over the others, probably, Lucas thought, by virtue of his position of authority within the group.

As the dinner progressed and the drinks flowed, the conversations became louder and more animated. Sheila, who was similar in age to Liz, was very adept at mimicry and amusing stories. On the other table, kindly Jane tried to involve the shy and bashful young Tim in discussions. On his own table, there was a lot of talk about favourite authors and books. Peter said he was an aficionado of Dostoevsky and Lucas made the others laugh by telling them that he had been trying to finish *War and Peace* for at least the last five years. Liz talked warmly about her favourite writer, Thomas Hardy while Sheila enthused over the novels of A. C. Benson, a writer unfamiliar to Lucas. It was a thoroughly lively discussion and Lucas had the very firm impression that these twentieth century aspiring writers read more often and more widely than most people from his own time.

At the end of the meal, Ed stood up and thanked them for their efforts throughout the term and told them that he was looking forward to reading the science fiction stories that they had handed in at the end of the last meeting. As they left the room, exchanging mutual festive wishes, Ed turned back to Lucas.

"Happy Christmas, Lucas!" he said, "And I am particularly looking forward to reading your story - I feel that it will tell me something really unusual....."

On the way back to Liz's flat, Lucas told her what Ed had

said to him. Liz laughed. "He just doesn't realise quite how unusual you are, Lucas!" she smiled.

Lucas spent a few minutes in the flat where Annette welcomed him warmly, insisting in providing him with a coffee. When he had left, Annette remarked to her daughter that she found Lucas such a charming and pleasant young man. Liz agreed with Annette's views, while rather ruefully reflecting that her mother was probably hoping that her daughter and Lucas might have a future as a couple.....

Chapter Three

Lucas had thought that it would be rather strange to spend Christmas day largely on his own, but he was glad he had volunteered to help the church wth providing the lunches for the less fortunate members of local society. With several other volunteers, he worked hard in the kitchen at the church hall before sitting down with them all to enjoy the traditional festive meal.

Back in his flat, Lucas spent a quiet evening. He turned up the heating, settled into the armchair and relaxed with the television on quietly in the background. The programmes he watched were lightweight and undemanding; he enjoyed the humour of *The Two Ronnies* and the comical mistakes occurring in various television programmes in Dennis Norden's *It'll Be Alright On The Night*. Later he thought about his family out there in the future and wondered what they were doing on Christmas Day 2081.

After his wonderful evening with Beth a few days later, Lucas spent New Year's Eve at a party in Lee given by one of the operatic society members, Graham. It was only a short walk to the house, and Lucas discovered that quite a few fellow members of the operatic society were among the large numbers of people at the gathering. It was an interesting evening, although of a different nature to the earlier party he had been to at Vernon's house. It was more of a conversational occasion - there was no dark room for dancing! - but Graham and Joanna's hospitality was superb. Of course, he missed Beth being there; the night before, she had explained that although they had been invited, Martin hadn't wanted to go.

However, he found the occasion enjoyable. Graham and Joanna's friends and neighbours were among the guests and there was quite an age range. He was introduced to several people, including a couple called Tom and Lynda who ran the Bluebird Cafe and recognised him from his various visits there. Later he was in a small group which featured a Southampton doctor where the discussion centred on the tragic emerging disease around the world which, as Lucas knew, would soon become known as "A.I.D.S." Some thought it would never become a pandemic, but the doctor was strongly of the opinion that it would be very serious and believed that the only cure that could be affective would be through the development of new vaccines. When the talk moved on to other matters, Lucas found himself wondering if this knowledgeable doctor would still be around forty years later to help deal with the infamous Coronavirus pandemic of the early twenties.

As he had experienced before, Lucas found it so very strange to know so much about the main events of the future. Another reminder of things to come occurred when Dennis, a lieutenant in the Royal Navy, introduced him to two Argentine naval officers who were in the country as part of a friendly visit to the area. In less than six months, he reflected, these friendly fellows would be seen as the enemy when the Falklands War would begin.

On the whole, Lucas found the party pleasant and quite relaxing. There was only one jarring episode when Belinda took him aside to say that many people in the operatic society were gossiping about him and Beth being too 'matey'. Lucas did not really know how to respond to this direct remark but Barry, who had happened to be standing nearby, had heard what Belinda had said.

"Don't worry, mate," he said, after Belinda had moved away, "touch of jealousy there, I reckon! You are the big attraction just now, you know!"

As midnight approached, Graham and Joanna called for all the guests to toast the New Year. When the clock struck twelve, Graham led them all outside onto the little street where they watched fireworks lighting up the sky. Some other neighbours also stepped outside to join them and there were mutual exchanges of good wishes for the new year. Not long afterwards, the party began to break up and Lucas walked the short distance home in the first hour of 1982. I won't see this whole year out here, he reflected, I have to return to my own time at the beginning of May. And I don't want to leave this life I have now, I really don't..... But he pulled himself together as he walked along these streets of a hundred years ago. There is still so much more time for me here, and I must live for the moment, he told himself. For who knows what 1982 will bring?

Chapter Four

The first three days of 1982 seemed to pass slowly. Lucas was longing to get on with his social life, and the next operatic society meeting was not until January 4th, with the Writers' Group re-starting on the 5th. He passed the time writing in his journals, idly watching television, listening to his tapes and records before springing into activity with a long run along the beach followed the next day by a swim at the Leisure Centre. At last it was Monday evening and he felt excited to being back to the normal routine as he drove to the rehearsal hall. It had only been a week since he had last seen Beth, but both of them were delighted to meet at the Vine for an early drink before the rehearsal.

"Happy New Year,Beth!" he cried as she emerged from her car.

"Same to you, Lucas!" she laughed as they walked arm-in-arm to the pub, "I wonder where we'll be and what we'll be doing this time next year!" Of course, Beth's light remark hit Lucas hard, but he managed to smile in return as they continued along the way.

Soon they were sitting together with their drinks. Lucas thought, happily, that the short time they had been away from each other had reinvigorated their affair. Among other things, they chatted about their respective Christmas experiences. While Beth had enjoyed seeing her relations, she admitted she felt happy to be back in the normal routine.

The rehearsal was bright and vigorous. Both Angela and Andrew were very pleased with the efforts of the chorus; the finale was practised for the first time and went particularly well. In the pub afterwards, everyone seemed to be in a happy frame of mind. Afterwards Beth came to sit in Lucas' car and soon the lovers were kissing and hugging with frenzy.

"Beth, come back to the flat!" gasped Lucas as they came up for air.

"Can't, it'll make me too late, but I'll come straight round on Thursday after principals' rehearsal," she promised.

Then she was gone, leaving Lucas rearranging his clothing before driving back to his flat with her lingering perfume to keep him company. Back there, with a sobering mug of hot chocolate, he reflected on the fact that the public performance of *H.M.S. Pinafore* was scheduled to take place during the very last week that he would be here before returning to his own time. Once more he wondered how on earth he would cope with leaving all this behind for ever.

Chapter Five

Next morning, Lucas drove to the Community Centre for the first meeting of his Writers' Circle in the New Year. As soon as the group had assembled, Ed, the tutor announced that he would set them all a task while he discussed with each of them in turn their science fiction stories which they had handed in before Christmas.

"I want each of you to write about the good and bad sides of Christmas. It can be general or personal in content. Once you have all got under way, I'll ask you one by one to come over to the quiet corner of the room to discuss your science fiction stories with me."

After a few minutes had passed, Tom was the first to be called out. Soon Lucas was enjoying the assignment. He wrote fluently first about the pleasures of Christmas - emphasizing the feelings of warmth and love engendered by the idea of the birth of Jesus and the sense of bringing light into the dark time of year. Meanwhile, Ed spent about ten minutes with each of the aspiring writers and just before coffee break time, called Lucas over to talk about his science fiction story.

"This is very good indeed, Lucas," Ed began. "I found the experiences of your character travelling back in time to the last century very intriguing."

He looked steadily at Lucas. "Tell me," he said, "do you

think time travel is a possibility? Because, for my part, it is something I would like to believe could happen. Your character in the story reacts to what has happened to him, what he sees, thinks and does, in a truly convincing way. Why, you have written this so well that it is almost as if you yourself have experienced travelling in time!"

And he sat back in his chair, waiting for Lucas to respond. Lucas realised that Ed had not spoken these words lightly - he knows about me, he thought. He responded carefully.

"Yes, Ed, I do believe that one day a device will be made that will enable us to travel through time," he said, looking steadily at the tutor. For one fleeting moment he was tempted to tell Ed the truth about himself but the feeling passed and the two sat silently for a moment.

Then Ed broke the tension. "Well, Lucas, I congratulate you on a first-rate story. And the next time you travel in time, include me with you!" And he stood up and called out, "Break time, everyone!"

In the refreshment room, Liz hurried to sit with Lucas and immediately asked him what Ed had thought about his story. Quietly he explained how the short interview had gone.

"I'm sure he senses that there really is something unusual going on. It wasn't just as a result of reading my story. Like you, Liz, he senses something. But I shan't tell him - nor anyone else - it will just be our secret." Liz briefly squeezed his hand.

"Thank you," she said, smiling. When they went back into the room after the break, Ed carried on calling out the remaining writers one by one. When it was Liz's turn, Lucas looked across with special interest. It seemed that Ed was impressed with her work too.

When Ed had finally seen each of them, he announced that next week they would discuss the work they had all done this morning.

"As for your science fiction stories, I would like each of you to exchange your own with another person to read and discuss with them at some time."

They all did as they were asked. Lucas handed his story to Jane, receiving hers in return, while Liz swapped hers with Peter. As usual now, Lucas and Liz went over to the White Hart for a little while and they agreed to spend a few minutes reading the stories they had received.

Jane's story was fun to read; she had imagined a space cruise ship of the future, and had described the various interactions of different people aboard. Peter, like Lucas, had written a time-travel piece; his protagonist had found himself suddenly transported it to the 30th century where everything around him was totally incomprehensible. They talked for a little while about Peter's tale.

"I expect I would find some things in your world very mystifying," Liz remarked. "And yet, here you are, here we are, in 1982, but in a few months' time, you will be living in another different year! It is so hard to comprehend..."

She looked across at him, her eyes moist. "I'll miss you so much, you old time-traveller!"

"Oh, Liz," he murmured, "I don't want to go back."

They sat holding hands for a moment in silence. Then Liz stood up to go, let go of his hands and smiled warmly at him.

"Lucas. You don't have to go back just yet. You still have time to live here. Make the most of every moment!" she said. "And there are still so many things I want you to tell me about!"

Chapter Six

And of course, it was only natural that many of the conversations that Liz and Lucas enjoyed during their next few meetings were about the changes the future would bring about. Many of the technologies that Lucas took for granted in 2081 were often a source of amazement to Liz. For example, she found it incredible that in this time everyone owned a small mobile device that could provide instant communication, with access to music, news, pictures, films and encyclopaedic information.

She heard about driverless cars, three-dimensional television, many cures for illnesses that had been so dangerous before and what Lucas described as "smart" technologies which controlled household utilities. But Lucas also told her that not everything had improved in the late twenty-first century. There were still great inequalities in life throughout the world. Lucas explained about "climate change" - a phrase unknown to Liz - and the disasters that ensued from this. And Liz was sad to hear that wars, weapons and the worship of militarism were, if anything, more rampant than in 1981.

Despite her curiosity and fascination with Lucas' descriptions of everyday life in 2081, it was quite clear to him that Liz had no real desire to actually visit the world of a century hence. As she explained to him, one day in his flat, she wanted her life to go forward on its normal course.

"I am very conscious, Lucas, that in a sense you are living two lives at the same time," she said to him one day. "And you have knowledge of how history will develop in the years after now."

"Yes, Liz, it is so strange in many ways," he replied, "but I am experiencing what, to me, is the past, in minute detail, on a day-to-day basis. I think that in a way, each day for me is a fresh start, like it is for you, Liz, and for everyone else here that I know."

She smiled warmly at him. "Well, it is marvellous for us to have this special and unique relationship! I'm special - and you're unique!!"

Chapter Seven

While his friendship with Liz proceeded in a comfortable fashion, the same could not be said about Lucas' relationship with Beth. Based as this was, to a large extent, on their mutual and powerful sexual attraction to each other, theirs was a volatile situation. It seemed to Lucas that Beth went through so many and varied emotions, As far as he was concerned, he always wanted to be with her and enjoy any opportunity for making love. Although there were times when he realised that he was being selfish, he found it difficult to understand how Beth could be on a massive high at one moment and then become cool and aloof towards him at another.

One rehearsal night at the end of January, she sat in his car at the end of the evening and told him, not for the first time, that their relationship must end. Yet on the following Monday, which was the occasion of the Annual General Meeting of the operatic society, she met him at the door of the rehearsal hall and urgently persuaded him to give the meeting a miss and take her out to the King's Head at Wickham. He could not resist. He did not care that she had changed her mind yet again.

They had a wonderful time together and ended up in bed at Lucas' flat. And so their on/off affair lurched along with so many highs and lows as the winter days gave way at last to the warmer weather of early spring. By this time, some of the rougher edges of their relationship were beginning to smooth out as they discovered that they could at last begin to develop more of a mutual interest in each other's broader hopes and desires in life. Lucas felt that a proper friendship was forming between them.

Chapter Eight

Lucas felt a sense of relief when the awful weather of this winter finally improved. He realised that Britain did not cope very well with snow and ice in the early 1980s. January had brought power cuts, frozen pipes, travel disruption and many other problems. Lucas thought that there was little, if any, planning to deal with severe weather at this time. Even down here on the south coast, road conditions were often so bad that he chose not to drive anywhere. Personally, he did not remember ever being so cold in his own time in the future, where the insidious actions of global climate change had meant that vicious winters were rare. To his annoyance, he had caught a cold in the last week of January - after he had taken some over-the-counter remedies, it went away quite quickly - but he was not accustomed to this type of illness, for by 2081 programmes of vaccination together with more careful and hygienic public behaviour had greatly reduced the prevalence of illnesses of this type.

As soon as he felt fitter again, he decided that it would be interesting to travel further afield. One Wednesday in the middle of February, the weather forecast promised a warmer than average day and he drove to Fareham station to take a train to London. It seemed strange to travel on the system that was still under national ownership. To him, the trains looked antiquated and shabby and the stations en route were drab and in need of investment. The diesel-electric multiple unit that took him to Eastleigh where he would change for a London train from Southampton was elderly and noisy, though not without a certain charm, he felt.

On the London train, he was pleased to see that there was plenty of room. This train consisted of ten coaches, something quite unfamiliar in the world of 2081, where trains, smarter and quicker as they had become, nevertheless crowded passengers into fewer carriages. His journey was pleasant enough and presently he was nearing the capital. When he had passed through the outlying places on the way, he had not particularly noticed too many differences from his own time but on the approach to Waterloo the views of grim factories, tatty warehouses and squalid housing brought the realisation to him that he was travelling in ancient times. The Waterloo terminus too, which he knew quite well in 2081, was almost unrecognisable. Here he stepped off the train into a large, gloomy place that was simply fulfilling its role as an arrival and departure point for travellers. The Waterloo that he knew was, by contrast, more like a bright shopping, food and entertainment centre.

Chapter Nine

What Lucas particularly wanted to visit today was the Social Science department of the University of London where he was studying in 2081. Would he even recognise it, he wondered as he ate a quick snack lunch in the Waterloo buffet. He decided to take the tube. He studied the underground map at the top of the stairs, discovering that the route to his destination - Russell Square - was the same as he knew in his own time, along the Northern Line to Leicester Square followed by the change onto the eastward arm of the Piccadilly Line. The corridors, stations and the trains themselves seemed scruffier, hotter and noisier than he was accustomed to in 2081, but the system was still basically the same, except for the fact that he and all the other passengers stood on the platform rather than behind a glass barrier when the train came in, and that there was a driver at the controls.

When he eventually alighted at Russell Square, Russell walked along a quite familiar road towards the University buildings, noting with some distaste the pollution emitting from the vast amount of diesel and petrol driven cars and lorries. He recognised the University buildings, although at this time there were less of them. Here was the Social Science department that he knew so well. It was a strange experience to walk around the place; he recognised some of the rooms, and the then-new lecture theatre, but the department was smaller than the version he worked in 2081. His own office was not here in 1982. The early twenty-first century addition to the main block was, of course, yet to happen. The fact that his room did not exist at this time made him feel very strange and discomfited. Even though he had mentally prepared himself for change, walking along among the groups of students in this familiar yet alien setting gave him a sense of unreality. Emerging from the building, he flopped down onto a seat on the lawn outside to recover his equanimity.

After a while, he walked along to a nearby cafe to have a refreshing cup of tea. His next plan was to go to another place he knew well in 2081 - Covent Garden. In his own time, this was a vibrant place, popular with tourists and Londoners alike with its mix of upmarket shops, restaurants, bars and entertainments of all kinds, together with the venerable transport museum and nearby theatres. But when Lucas emerged from the tube station, Covent Garden looked very different. It appeared to be in a state of transition - Lucas knew the actual fruit market had been relocated some years before 1982 - and most of the fine old buildings stood empty. There were just a few small shops and a couple of bars, although at least the then-new London Transport Museum was there. After the original market had closed, there had been plans to demolish the fine old buildings during the late 1970s, but fortunately preservation groups had won the day and provided the starting point for the attractive Covent Garden area that Lucas knew in the twenty-first century.

Lucas made his way back to Waterloo in the late afternoon. As he sat in the train on the way back home, he felt rather melancholy. For some reason, his visit to London in 1982 had made him feel isolated and lonely, more than at any other time since he had left his own century.

He talked about all of this to Liz a few evenings later, when he met her in the bar of The Alverbank. There was no-one else there, and they were able to talk together in comfort. Lucas found it comforting to confide his thoughts to Liz, even though, as she said, she could only guess what it must be like for him in his unique position, fixed as she was in her normal real time. By the end of the evening, he felt much better, for he knew he could always rely on Liz for support and friendship.

Chapter Ten

For the next few weeks, life settled into a reasonably regular routine for Lucas - that is, if living each day as a traveller from a hundred years in the future could ever be a routine affair. Rehearsals for the forthcoming production of *H.M.S. Pinafore* continued on a weekly basis, as did the Writers' Circle group. Lucas also visited the leisure centre quite often and kept up with his running exercise. He went to watch a couple of Gosport Borough football matches at Privett Park, once in the company of Barry from the operatic society.

He saw Liz frequently. Their reciprocal friendship was, he realised, a vital part of his life. Theirs was a platonic relationship and he felt that both of them were content to keep things that way between them. With Beth, of course, it was a different matter. Lucas resigned himself to her frequent changes of mind about carrying on with their sexual affair. But when she was in the mood for fun, he was always ready to join in. When their passion was in full flow, everything felt so good and he was more than happy to go along for the ride. What was more, when they found time to talk, he discovered what a complex and many-sided person she was; like Liz, she had always believed that there was more to life than the everyday routines, and she too had written stories from time to time. Lucas encouraged her to write some more for him to read and decided that he would give her a copy of his own time-travel tale.

Thus it was that one evening in March, when Lucas had driven Beth out to their favourite Wickham pub, they spent most of their time there reading each other's stories. Beth's tale was written in the first person, and concerned her relationship with a man whom she had met at a party. In the story, she and the other man met frequently in quite exotic locations. Much of her narrative related her thoughts and feelings, and how she prepared herself mentally and physically for meeting the man. It was very well written and Lucas told Beth he thought it was really interesting. She blushed with pleasure at his enthusiastic praise. She had guessed of course that he would see some elements of their own affair in the story, although the man she had portrayed was not intended to be Lucas, but rather a more romantic, almost perfect Adonis.

In her turn, Beth was impressed with Lucas' time travel tale.

"I like this, Lucas!" she said brightly. "I can picture your hero and his adventures in the past. I'd love to go back in time and see how things really were in the nineteenth century!"

They spent the rest of the evening talking about their stories. Lucas felt that they were experiencing a pleasing companionship. Tonight there was no sexual tension. When they parted, Beth gave Lucas a hug and a chaste kiss.

"This has been a very different sort of evening, Lucas," she said, "Thank you for sharing your thoughts with me."

Chapter Eleven

It had been a very different sort of evening. Lucas
realised that Beth, unlike Liz and Ed, had not sensed
his unique position in this world, even after reading his
time traveller story. This was a relief to him. It made it
easier for the two of them to continue their relationship
on a more comfortable level. These days, they were regarded
as a steady couple by the other members of the society.
Meanwhile other pairings and groups ebbed and
flowed. For example, Belinda and Mike, a rather quiet
member of the chorus, became close, while Jacqueline,
the pianist, became very flirtatious with Vernon. Yet for
all the changing social interactions within the group,
Lucas could sense the strong unanimity as everyone
pulled together during rehearsals towards the ultimate
presentation of the show. Lucas had already realised, of
course, that the performances of *H.M.S. Pinafore* would
be taking place in the week before he was due to return
to his own time.

Meanwhile Lucas carried on attending the Writers'
Circle. Here was a different dynamic compared to the
operatic society. Each member strove to improve his
or her own writing, heeding the expert of advice of the
tutor. There were some one-to-one friendships among the
group - Liz and Lucas, for instance - but on the whole,
each person was working towards the goal of becoming
a decent writer. Ed, the tutor, had suggested early in
the spring term that each of them should submit one of

their short stories to a variety of magazines and other publications to see if their efforts would be rewarded. One day in early April, just after they had assembled for the session, Ed asked Tim to announce some news. The young man stood up.

"I've had my story accepted by *Shoreline Of Infinity* magazine," he said, rather diffidently. "It was the one I wrote for our class assignment before Christmas. I amended it a little, and it will appear in the July issue."

There were murmurs of appreciation from the others and, blushing, Tim sat down again.

"We all congratulate you, Tim, " said Ed. "If you don't know the magazine, it's a quality one that specialises in science fiction stories, publishing four times a year. Let's get Tim to read it to us!"

Tim read out his story. It concerned the adventures of a young man of 25 who had joined an exploration group in Virginia in the United States which was studying part of the Luray Caverns. One day, he went off on his own to explore a more remote section of the caves. At one point, he was sure he heard strange singing or chanting sounds. Mystified, he tried to locate the music, but to no avail. Eventually, he made his way back to the base camp. To his alarm, he felt inexplicably tired and really found it a struggle to walk back. When he finally arrived, he collapsed, exhausted, into his tent, wondering if somehow he had picked up some kind of illness or injury along the way. But it was much worse than this. Looking down at his hands, he saw to his horror that they looked gnarled and aged. He picked up a mirror. The face that looked back at him was just about recognisable as his own. It was now the face of an old man...

It was obvious that everyone in the group was impressed with Tim's tale. After the class had dispersed, Lucas and Liz went along to the White Hart as usual and they discussed the story that they had heard. They agreed that one of the most compelling aspects of young Tim's writing was his ability to anticipate how it might feel to be old.

"Well, one day we shall all know what it will be like," reflected Liz, "but it will take much longer for you to achieve old age, Lucas - relatively speaking, that is!"

"I see what you mean, Liz!" smiled Lucas. "And in a way, I suppose, the moral of Tim's story might be that we should make the most of every moment that is granted to us!"

Chapter Twelve

During the next few days, as his day of departure came ever closer, Lucas tried hard to cherish every minute. He revisited some of the places and events that he had experienced during the last five months; the car boot sale, football at Privett Park, even the next show put on by the Gosport Players. On Easter Sunday he joined the large congregation at the main service at Alverstoke church. Afterwards, once again he shook hands with the Vicar - and, as before, he knew that the clergyman sensed that there was something strange about Lucas' presence. This time, the vicar said a few words that affected Lucas strongly.

"Thank you for coming here again." he said, looking straight into Lucas' eyes. "We shall not see you here again, I feel. You will be going far, far away. But wherever you are going, young man, God's blessings go with you." And then he turned to greet the next people leaving the church, while Lucas walked away, full of emotion.

Later, as he sat eating lunch in the Old Lodge, Lucas wondered yet again how it was that only certain people he had met - the vicar, Liz and Ed - had sensed the mystery about him. But Beth did not appear to have felt that there was anything particularly odd about him, even though they had been so intimate. His thoughts turned to something very important that he must achieve very soon now - he must tell Beth that he would be leaving after the opera week came to an end. Just now, he did not think that Beth would be able to cope with learning the actual truth about himself. He felt he would have to fall back on the excuse that he would have to go back to live in London to complete his studies. Moreover, he would also have to tell his other friends in the operatic group that he wouldn't be seeing them again. Such thoughts put him into a melancholy mood. He had grown so close to these people over the months; he had embraced the vitality and spirit of the times. Sometimes he found it very hard to believe that his real life must carry on, not here, but in 2082, But he had to return to his own times.

Chapter Thirteen

Time was moving forward inexorably. As the days got longer, Lucas' remaining time in 1982 became shorter. On the Wednesday of the week before *H.M.S. Pinafore* was due to take place, the cast and chorus were asked to come down to the Bogue Hall to collect and try on their costumes for the show. Jillian, the wardrobe mistress together with her helpers, checked the fittings for each of them. There was some lively banter, particularly among the men, as they appeared in unfamiliar clothes, some of which needed quite a few adjustments. At one point, Beth, wearing her elegant outfit for her role as the Captain's daughter, Josephine, came over to Lucas who was looking at himself in the long mirror and adjusting his sailor's garb.

"I like you in that outift, Lucas," she smiled. "I can always go for a man in uniform!"

"Why, thank you ma'am!" he laughed, "And you look gorgeous too! Don't you think it's interesting to see all these folks who we see at all the other times in normal clothes, suddenly transformed into different characters!"

Beth agreed. "I love this time, just before we start the show. It's going to be a good week Lucas! You'll love it, especially as it's the first time you've been on stage!"

As she turned away to talk to Jacqueline, Lucas,

surrounded by the lively chatter of these people he had come to know so well, fervently wished he could not only enjoy the fun of the show but carry on seeing everyone again when it was over.

The very next evening was to be a complete run-through of *H.M.S. Pinafore*, the last practice before the Dress Rehearsal on the following Monday. Later on during the costume evening, Lucas had asked Beth to meet him before the rehearsal for a drink in the Vine. It was high time, he had decided, to tell Beth that he wouldn't be around after the show was over. It would be so hard, but it must be done.

As soon as they were settled with their drinks on this Thursday evening, Lucas, full of trepidation, broke the news to Beth that he would not be around any more after the opera week was over because of his University commitments in London. She was silent while he was explaining. He could not tell how she was taking the bad news. But when she did respond, she seemed calm enough.

"You know I will miss you, Lucas. Won't you perhaps be able to come down and see us all here, at least occasionally? But - I want you to know - we've had some fabulous times together, haven't we? It's been great. But maybe it's better for us to end this way......"

Her voice trailed off and Lucas, tears pricking at his eyes, reached across the table to take her hands in his.

"Oh Beth. I shall miss you so much - knowing you has

made my life wonderful..." he began, but she squeezed his hands hard and interrupted.

"No pining now, Lucas, no sad faces. We've got a show to put on and look forward to!"

And so the former lovers gathered up their things and walked together into the rehearsal hall.

That night, the run-through of the show went very well. One part of Lucas' mind enjoyed the excitement of the rehearsal, but mostly his thoughts kept straying to the sad situation in which he had placed both Beth and himself. In the Vine afterwards however, Beth seemed bright enough. When he told the others that next week's show would be his one and only appearance on the stage, it was obvious to him that he would be missed. Barry, Vernon, Bob and many of his friends expressed sincere regrets that he wouldn't be around any more.

By the time he arrived back at his flat, Lucas felt deflated and depressed. How hard it was going to be to have to give up this life that had been so good to him.

Chapter Fourteen

Nevertheless, he had to move on. There were practicalities to sort out before he could travel back to his own time. He had already given notice to vacate his flat, and he would of course leave behind the extra furniture he had bought himself. He made a present of the Fiesta to Liz, who was just about to start having driving lessons. She was so happy to take it, for it would always have a special association for her in the future. He began to sort out the various things he had bought over the last few months, deciding which ones he could fit into his suitcases. Some of these items - his Walkman and the tapes he had bought - would become valuable old relics when he returned to the twenty first century, but of course, and much more important, they would hold so much sentimental value for him. He would take some of the newspapers and magazines he had bought, together with the stories that Liz and Beth had shared with him.

On that last weekend before he had to leave, he had the bright idea of buying a Polaroid camera so that he could take photographs during the show of the people he had come to know so well. The very last thing he bought was a little bottle of the perfume that Beth always used. One day, an old man, in the far distant future, he would open the bottle and the fragrance would bring back a beautiful memory of Beth from those long ago days.

On Sunday morning, Lucas drove to the Bogue Hall

to take part in what was known as "Band Call", when the orchestra came along for the first time to practice the show together with the principals and any chorus members who wished to be there. Beth had told Lucas that this particular event was always exciting and uplifting after all the weeks of rehearsals with just piano accompaniments. Soon the rehearsal was under way with Andrew conducting and Lucas found it fascinating to see how the orchestra and soloists adjusted and re-rehearsed until the music flowed along in style. Somehow the sharper sounds of the band enhanced the music he knew so well and he was glad he had come. The soloists, particularly Beth who was in fine voice, performed well. He knew it was gong to be a successful show. When the session ended, Lucas walked back with Beth to their cars and as they parted, she gave him a quick peck. "It's gong to be a great show week, Lucas!" she said brightly. "Let's have lots of fun! See you tomorrow at Dress Rehearsal!"

Chapter Fifteen

When Lucas awoke next morning, one of the first thoughts that came into his head was this would be the very last Monday he would know in 1982. Quickly he put this negative notion to the back of his mind. In the morning he went down to the Library and took Liz along to their cafe in her break. Once they had settled there, he gave her her ticket to see the show on Thursday.

"Wait for me after the opera's finished, and I'll take you over to The Vine to meet all the others. Then I'll run you home afterwards," he said.

"It'll be fun seeing you on the stage and all these folks you've told me about, particularly Beth," she smiled. "I hope she won't mind you bringing me!"

Lucas assured her that there wouldn't be any problem - he had told Beth all about his friendship with Liz. As they drank their coffee, their conversation was light and positive; they mostly talked about the show. Both steered clear of mentioning the subject of Lucas' departure after the opera was over. Presently Liz rose to go back to the library.

"I'll see you on Thursday evening, Lucas," she said. "Good luck! I'll be thinking of you, And make sure you enjoy every moment!"

Smiling, she squeezed his hand and left. Lucas sat on for a little while longer, lost in his own thoughts, before walking along the High Street to have lunch in the Wimpy. Taking advantage of the lovely May weather, he spent some time relaxing in the Ferry Gardens. For once, the afternoon passed slowly and he became impatient for the time to come for the Dress Rehearsal to start.

At last he was making his way to the Bogue Hall. When he arrived, all was bustle and excitement. In the changing rooms below stage, he dressed himself in his sailor's garb before going in to the make-up room where Lorraine applied the necessary cosmetics. It was quite strange, Lucas thought, to see his altered face looking back at him from the mirror. Promptly at half past seven, all the chorus members and the principal performers were ready to begin. Waiting on the stage behind the curtains with the men's chorus, Lucas felt a thrill of anticipation as the orchestra played the first notes of the overture.

Exciting as it was to perform in the opera with the orchestra for the first time, Lucas knew that the Dress Rehearsal was not exactly a total success. Calvin, in the role of the hero Ralph, forgot some of his words in his first song. Bob, who was playing Sir Joseph Porter, had difficulties with his wig which kept slipping to one side. At one point in the show, some of the men's chorus failed to get onto the stage at the right time and then the stage lights failed in the middle of the finale. Andrew insisted on the chorus re-singing a couple of numbers. At last the rehearsal ended and both Andrew and Angela called the whole cast back onto the stage to talk about some of the failings. But, as Angela reminded them all, there was an old theatre saying that a bad dress rehearsal meant that the performances for the public would be a great success.

It had been a long rehearsal. By the time Lucas had finished taking off his make-up and joined some of the others in the pub, there was barely time to have a drink. He was disappointed that Beth had chosen not to come over to The Vine tonight, but, as Barry pointed out, for the rest of the week the opera ought to finish round about half past nine and so they would have plenty of time for relaxation.

Chapter Sixteen

Next morning, Lucas felt a sense of great excitement at the prospect of performing the show in front of an audience. He put on his tape of *H.M.S. Pinafore* and sang along with it. He ate lunch in the Penguin cafe and then went into the bookshop on High Street and chose some 'Good Luck' cards to give to the principals - a tradition in the operatic society. He reminded himself to take his new Polaroid camera with him tonight so that he could take some photographs backstage.

He arrived at the Bogue Hall in good time to sort out his costume and have his make-up applied. Naturally there was a sense of excitement and anticipation in the air tonight. Lucas had time to hand out his good luck cards and managed to take a few photographs of some of the cast in their costumes. Most of his subjects were impressed to see the pictures from the instant camera. How amazed they would be, Lucas thought wryly, if they could imagine a device from the next century which could take as many photos as one wished and display them on its screen immediately! Of course he took two pictures of Beth in her costume, one for her and the other for him to have as a keepsake.

As the time approached half past seven, the hall was full. The orchestra played the first notes of the overture and *H.M.S. Pinafore* was soon sailing along merrily. Just as Angela had predicted, the show went brilliantly. Lucas felt full of vitality and delight to be performing for an appreciative and enthusiastic audience. Time seemed to fly past; the curtain descended to cheers and applause and the first night came to a successful end. It was a happy and bubbling group that hurried along to "The Vine" afterwards. Tonight, some of the members of the group had friends and family who had come to see the opera and quite of few of them came over to the pub. Beth's Aunt and Uncle were there, Bob had two friends from work, Theresa's boy friend was there too. Towards the end of the evening, Lucas managed to spend a quick moment alone with Beth. Impulsively he whispered to her, "Come to the flat one night!"

"I'll have to think about it," she demurred, "I'll let you know tomorrow!" and she squeezed his hand briefly before going back to her relatives.

Driving back at the end of the evening, Lucas felt full of excitement. Even though he knew his renewed burst of desire for Beth had been partially fuelled by the thrill of being in the show, and even the two of them had more or less 'closed down' their affair because he was leaving, he knew he wanted to have one last loving time with her.

Chapter Seventeen

In the night Lucas had a vivid dream. Unsurprisingly *H.M.S. Pinafore* was the setting, but instead of being in the chorus he was taking the part of Ralph, the hero. In his dream, the performance was taking place in an enormous stadium with a massive audience who sang along with all the music. A huge spotlight was upon him and Beth as they performed their duet in Act One. But as soon as he left the stage he discovered that he could not remember a single thing that he was supposed to say at his next entrance.

Beth whispered something to him - but he could not understand what it was - and in an instant the stage, the audience and the theatre were gone and he stood alone on top of a hill. At this point he woke up in a sweat, thinking that what he had just dreamt was absolutely real.

He lay in bed for a while, trying to remember the details of his dream, but the memory was fading fast. Did it mean anything, he wondered, or was the whole thing just the result of the impact that being in the opera had had on him?

As he went through the day, performing the necessary household tasks, fragments of that dream kept intruding upon him. But at last it was time to get ready for tonight's performance. Tonight there was to be an extra event, as every Wednesday in show week it had become a tradition for many of the group members and any of their guests to go out after the performance for a late celebratory dinner at the T & J Chinese Restaurant. As it happened, two of Lucas' Writers' Circle - Mary and Ed, the tutor, together with his wife Jennifer, were coming to watch the show.

Chapter Eighteen

Lucas felt that the opera performance was not quite as good as it had been on the previous night, with a few fluffed lines and occasional lapses in the chorus singing. Nevertheless the audience were enthusiastic and once more Lucas felt the sheer excitement of being on stage. When the show was over, he quickly removed his make-up and hurried outside to meet his guests. Mary had enjoyed the opera, but decided not to stay on for the Chinese meal, but Ed and Jennifer were happy to come along. Entering the restaurant they sat down at one of the tables which had been moved together to accommodate the large group from the society. Soon everyone had arrived and Lucas was pleased to see that Beth, in the company of Heather, Louise, Belinda and her husband, found seats opposite him on the same table.

The waiters did a marvellous job. Serving up the many different orders of food and drink for the large group. Lucas introduced Ed and Jennifer to the people sitting near him and soon Ed was chatting confidently to Andrea who was on his left, while Lucas found Jennifer a lively and flirtatious presence. He learnt that she was a member of a local theatrical group which performed Shakespeare plays during the summer at a variety of venues. Reluctantly he had to decline Jennifer's invitation to see her playing Cleopatra in July, explaining that he would be back in London by then. "Perhaps another time, then?" she suggested, looking rather meaningfully at him. She really is a very attractive woman, Lucas reflected and for a few moments his train of thought ran along regretful lines that this exciting and promising life was about to end so abruptly.

A few minutes later, Beth got up to visit the loo upstairs. Lucas knew he had to speak to her privately and a moment or two later he went upstairs too. She did not seem surprised to see him waiting for her. Impulsively he took her into his arms and they kissed, briefly but passionately.

"Beth, you will come to the flat one more time before I leave, won't you?" he implored. To his delight she nodded.

"I'll come on Friday, straight after the show!" she said a little breathlessly, before squeezing his hand and hurrying off down the stairs

Not long afterwards, the meals and drinks were finished and the group began to break up. Outside, Ed and Jennifer took their leave of Lucas. Jennifer gave him a warm hug and Ed shook hands firmly.

"Goodbye, Lucas. It's been great having you in our Writers' Circle. I hope you'll remember your time with us."

"Thanks Ed for everything!" replied Lucas warmly. "It's been a pleasure!"

"So - good luck old fellow - wherever you're going in the

future!" And Ed turned quickly and was gone.

Much later that night, when Lucas had had a bath and retired to bed, his thoughts whirled to and fro - the joys and excitement he had experienced this week being counterbalanced by the sadness of having to leave it all behind.

Chapter Nineteen

Lucas spent most of the next day writing. He tidied up his report. He read through everything he had written in the last six months, using his special skills to arrange his observations into an analytical, academic form. When he had finished this work, he took out his personal journal and read this thoroughly too before adding some more comments on the show week. How long ago some of the events he had described in his early time here seemed now! So many lovely memories......

The day passed quite quickly and he began to get ready for the third night of *H.M.S. Pinafore*. Liz was coming to see the show tonight and he had promised to take her over to The Vine afterwards so that she could meet the opera people he had often talked about to her.

Tonight the performance was better than it had been on Wednesday. Once again, it seemed to Lucas, that it was over all too soon. He still felt full of energy despite all the singing and dancing - he felt he could go on doing this for ever. After changing, he hurried out to meet Liz who was waiting for him by the main door. She was full of praise for the opera and to his pleasure told him that she was proud to be friends with someone who could perform so well on the stage! They walked along to The Vine and Lucas introduced Liz to all the people he knew.

After he had bought a round of drinks, he was pleased

to see that Beth had drawn up an extra chair so that Liz could sit at the same table with the usual group of friends. Soon Liz was chatting cheerfully to Beth, Belinda and Patricia. Lucas fell into conversation with Barry, Bob and Vernon. The latter asked him about his social studies project and what he was going to do when he returned to London. Lucas explained that he had written about belonging to his two societies, with an emphasis on the social and psychological effects that he had observed. The three men were interested in what he had to say.

"So - we're all part of your account?" asked Bob, "Hope you've only written nice things about us!"

"Tell you what, Lucas," exclaimed Barry, "if what you've written becomes a best-seller in the academic field, send us a free copy at some time!"

They went on talking about Lucas' work for some time, laughing at the thought that he might have included some scandalous gossip about the parties and affairs he had been observing in the last six months.

A little later, when the conversation had turned to discussing aspects of the show, Lucas noticed that neither Liz nor Beth were there for the moment. Their glasses were empty and he took the opportunity to go up to the bar with Barry to buy another round.

"Those two have been gone for a long time," he remarked to Barry as they were waiting to be served. "Probably discussing clothes, you know what women are like!" laughed Barry.

Just at this point, Liz and Beth came back into the bar. I wonder what they have been talking about, Lucas thought. As he set their drinks before them, he noticed that both of them looked rather serious. Quickly however, Beth recovered her composure and soon they were talking with the other women in a light-hearted way.

When the landlord called "Time!", Liz went over to the buy cigarettes from the vending machine in the corner. While she was doing this, Lucas was able to whisper "Tomorrow?" to Beth and she gave him a smile and a thumbs-up sign.

Lucas drove Liz back to his flat. On the way she chatted brightly about the evening.

"It was great to meet all your friends," she said, "I can see why you've enjoyed being in the group."

"I wonder what you made of them all - particularly Beth? I noticed you had a really long chat with her - what did you talk about all that time?"

Liz smiled to herself. "Oh, you know, all sorts of stuff - the show, some of the people and a few other things."

"Did I get a mention?" asked Lucas.

"Ah well, your name might have come up," she laughed.

Back in the flat, Lucas made coffees and the sat silently for a few minutes. The overwhelming realisation had come over Lucas that this would be the last time they would ever spend in each other's company. He turned to Liz, tears in his eyes.

"Hush, Lucas. We both know what's about to happen. You know you must go back to live your life in your own time."

"It's just so hard, Liz," he said tearfully. "And even though I've tried to prepare myself for this......" And as he trailed off, Liz bent forward to take his hands in hers.

"Lucas. Of course this is difficult for you. And for me as well, But....we both have separate lives ahead of us. And there are so many good and wonderful things waiting for you when you jump forward to your own time. That life, that you have left behind for the last six months, is waiting for you to start up again. In 2082 you have family, friends and a style of living that I can only imagine. And - I'm sure there are some things from 1982 that you will definitely be glad to see the back of!"

This last sentence made Lucas smile and while they finished their coffees, they both relaxed and began talking about the tonight's show. Finally Liz said she must go now and Lucas drove her back to Seaward Towers. It was quiet and still by the harbour as they walked to the entrance. At the lift they shared hugs and a long kiss. When it arrived, they gazed steadily at each other for one last time.

"Goodbye, Lucas," she whispered. "How lucky I am to have known someone who makes saying farewell so hard."

And she stepped into the lift and was gone. Lucas returned to the car and sat there full of emotion. Just as he turned the ignition key, a light came on high up in the building. Liz was waving to him as he drove away.

Chapter Twenty

Lucas went straight to bed as soon as he returned to his flat. Rather to his surprise, he slept soundly that night, waking quite late on what was to be his last full day in the place he had known as home for the last few months. Tomorrow, he had booked in to The Alverbank again for one more night before his return to the twenty-first century on Sunday morning.

It was time to say some farewells. First he had a long chat with Geoff, who ran the post office and shop downstairs. He felt inordinately pleased when Geoff praised him as having been a model tenant. Next he went to Curzons, the hairdressing establishment to say goodbye to Aureole who had cut and styled his hair every three weeks since December. Finally he visited his two favourite Lee cafés, the Penguin and the Bluebird to offer his thanks and take his leave.

Each parting filled him with sadness. He went to sit on a bench overlooking the sea in the bright May morning, full of thoughts and memories. At last he returned to the flat to get ready for the penultimate performance of the opera. Tonight, after the show, Beth would be coming. And even though this would be for the last time, the prospect still filled him with excitement.

"It's going to be a good night tonight," remarked Bob to Lucas while they were changing before the show. "It always goes well on the Fridays!"

Bob was right. Backed by a lively and enthusiastic audience, the show rattled along at a great pace. Soloists, chorus and orchestra were in perfect harmony and when the final curtain fell there were shouts of approval from the watching concertgoers. As they left the theatre, Beth sought out Lucas.

"You go back to the flat, Lucas? I'd better stay for just one drink with the others - or they'll think it strange that neither of us is at The Vine tonight. I'll come as quick as I can!" she promised.

Lucas agreed that this was a sensible plan and so drove straight back to the flat. This would be the last time, he reflected, that he would ever be alone with Beth. He would see her at the after show party tomorrow, of course, but as she had told him already, her husband Martin would be with her. He tidied up, poured himself a glass of wine and put on his favourite E.L.O. record, *Time*. Half an hour later, he heard Beth's light footsteps on the stairs. He threw open the door to welcome her. He thought she had never looked so enticing. She was still on a high from being one of the stars of the show and exuded an exciting mixture of perfume and alcohol. Somehow there was no need for any talking. They fell upon each another in a frenzy of sexual passion, before falling onto the bed. Their love-making was quick and passionate. Finally they lay together, warm and happy.

"Lovely girl, I didn't even have time to offer you a glass of wine!", said Lucas, "would you like one now?"

"No, I'd better not," she smiled. "I had two in the pub before I came, and I drank those quickly! Can you make me a coffee, please? And I'd better get up while you do that - as usual (and you've heard me say this so often) I mustn't be late!"

While they were drinking their coffees, both were quiet. At last Beth rose to leave.

"Lucas," she said quietly, "I'm not one for big dramatic farewells. I know we won't meet again - not in this way - but...but...I just want you to know that it's been wonderful."

Lucas was tearful as he looked at this woman who had meant so much to him.

"Beth. I don't want to go away from you. I shall remember every time we have had together. Always."

"Me too," she said hoarsley. "Thank you....."

And she turned away so that he would not see that she was crying a little. They walked down to her car and shared one deep and loving kiss before she drove away.

Alone now, Lucas sat quietly for along time, his thoughts too deep for tears, before retiring to the bed that still retained the warm scents of his lover. At last he fell into a dreamless sleep.

Chapter Twenty-one

Here it was - the day of the last performance of the opera and the final time he would see all those people he had got to know so well. Practicalities got him through the day. He packed his case, plus the extra large holdall to accommodate several of the things he had bought during his time here. Of course, he had to leave behind the many extra items of furniture and decoration with which he had brightened up the flat. Soon the place would have a new tenant. What adventures would he or she have in this place, he wondered.

He drove to The Alverbank and booked in for his final night. He had asked for his original room there, and soon he was sitting there in the same place where his journey had begun back in the cold winter days of November. He had a late lunch and prepared for the last show.

At the Hall, as usual, all was bustle and a sense of excitement. His dark mood began to improve. I am determined to do my best to enjoy every minute and finish my time here on a high note, he thought to himself.

Once more, the show went well. For one final time, Lucas sang lustily with the chorus. All the principal singers were on top of their form. From the wings, Lucas watched Beth perform her opening song. How poised and professional she was, he thought; I shall always remember these special moments. All too soon, Lucas was singing the last chorus of *H.M.S. Pinafore* together with the whole company. The curtain fell to cheers and applause from the audience. After a few seconds it rose again to reveal the whole group of performers on the stage and Michael, the Chairman, delivered his customary address. He offered his thanks to all concerned in the production and invited the audience to come and see the society's next production of *The Yeomen Of the Guard* which was to be performed in November. Where shall I be in November, thought Lucas. What shall I be doing then?

After he had changed, removed his make-up and handed in his sailor's costume, Lucas waited a little while until most of the group had left. He walked alone into the hall, empty now, and looked across to the stage, This was the last time he would see this place that he had come to know so well. Sighing, he made his way to his car and began the drive to Angela's house in Fareham where the after-show party was to be held.

All those familiar faces were there. He did his best to join in with the light-hearted chatter, although he sensed that perhaps there was something of a feeling of disappointment among others too that the show week was over, But, he reflected sadly, at least they would be working on a new production almost at once, whereas he would be denied such a renewal.

Time passed quickly as Lucas exchanged his last words with many of the friends he had come to know so well. Eventually he stepped outside into the garden and looked up at the bright stars - the same ones that he would be seeing a century later in just a few short hours.

He was alone for only a minute or two. Here came Beth to greet him for one last time. They hugged each other closely. She was very subdued.

"Goodbye, Lucas," she whispered, "I must leave you now. But...here...take this."

She placed an envelope into his hand.

"It's just a little letter for you from me. But!" And she stepped back to gaze at him steadily. "But! You must promise me faithfully - please - that you will not read it until...until you have left. Promise."

She could speak no more. Lucas kissed her tenderly.

"I promise. Beth. For ever and always I will remember you and those wonderful times we had...."

She squeezed his hand once more and left him, turning around at the door to give him a brave smile. He stood still for a while, holding the letter with its faint imprint of Beth's perfume. He would do as she had asked. He would read her words and thoughts later - a hundred years later......

Chapter Twenty-two

Not long after this, Lucas said his goodbyes as he prepared to leave the party. By a strange coincidence, the last man he spoke to was Andrew, the Musical Director, who had been the first person he had met on the evening he joined the operatic group last November.

Driving back to the hotel, Lucas felt a strange sort of emptiness. Unexpectedly, he had a decent night's sleep. And now, here it was - his last day here in 1982. He performed his necessary tasks and went down to breakfast, which he hardly tasted. It was as though his emotions had closed down after all the overload of feelings that had beset him for the last few days. He paid his bill and walked outside with his suitcase and bags. Still feeling numb he took out his Mallett device. Its figures indicated that there were just five minutes to go before his transfer back to the future would take place - 12.00, Sunday 9th May. He went to stand as close as he remembered to the spot where he had arrived last November. He breathed deeply and shaded his eyes from the mid-day sun and took one last look out at the bay beyond the little bridge.

There were several people out and about on this fine day. But at the point where the narrow path met the main road, he saw two women standing close together. Beth and Liz were waving to him!

Lewis gasped in amazement, emotion rushing through

him. He just had time to wave back frantically and call out their names before darkness descended for a moment. Then he was regenerated into his own time, still waving and calling as the black car from the Institute appeared to take him away.

Chapter Twenty-three

A little later, back at the Institute, Lucas was granted some time to be alone in a quiet room to help him readjust and recover before undergoing various physical and mental tests that were deemed necessary on his return from the past. From the inside pocket of his jacket, he took out Beth's letter and read the words she had written a hundred years ago.

Dear Lucas,

It is so strange to be sending you a letter that you will not read tomorrow, but some time in the far distant future instead. Yes, I know where you are going. Liz told me the truth about you when I talked with her on Thursday. I found it so hard to believe but eventually she convinced me.

Lucas, now I think back, the fact that you are from another time explains some of the odd things about you! (Although as you know very well, I always thought you were cool and attractive!!). But I think you could have told me - or perhaps not? I wonder, if you had explained it all to me, whether it would have made any difference to our relationship.

But I want you to know that this has been a wonderful time for me. For the rest of my life, I will remember all the fun we had together so often. Of course, in the rest of our lives, I suppose both of us will know many other people, perhaps other lovers. I just hope you will never forget me.

I wish you didn't have to go. I shall miss you so. And Lucas - when you are reading these words I shall be long gone. So I want you to remember and picture me just as I am right now.

Goodbye my friend. Sending you so much love across the years. Have a great life.

Beth. xx

p.s. I hope you will see me - and Liz - for a moment before you leave us for your own time. We will be there to with our smiles and love to send you on your way.